LIMBO

LIMBO

·

A NOVEL BY
DIXIE SALAZAR

WHITE PINE PRESS · FREDONIA, NY

This is a work of fiction. Names, characters, places, and incidents are either the
product of the author's imagination or are used fictitiously. Any resemblance to
actual persons, living or dead, events, or locales is entirely coincidental.

Publication of this book was made possible, in part,
by grants from the National Endowment for the Arts
and the New York State Council on the Arts.

Author's Acknowledgements:
I would like to thank all of my teachers and the friends who have
supported me in my work. A special thanks to Steve Yarbrough
for his generous help and encouragement.

Cover painting by Dixie Salazar

Book design by Elaine LaMattina

First Edition

Manufactured in the United States of America.

ISBN 0-1877727-45-8

9 8 7 6 5 4 3 2 1

White Pine Press
10 Village Square • Fredonia, NY 14063

LIMBO

For my family —
and for Jon.

LIMBO

Home is where one starts from. As we grow older
The world becomes stranger, the pattern more complicated
Of dead and living. Not the intense moment
Isolated, with no before and after,
But a lifetime burning in every moment
And not the lifetime of one man only
But of old stones that cannot be deciphered.
There is a time for the evening under starlight,
A time for the evening under lamplight
(The evening with the photograph album) . . .
In my end is my beginning.

— T.S. Eliot
Four Quartets

LIMBO

Chapter 1
·
Fresno, California

A cracked toilet squatted in the front yard, a few burnt marigolds, straggling from the bowl. "Constipated marigolds," Cassiopeia thought as she stepped over stiff rolls of sun-burnt newspapers. The street felt creepy, "One of Ned's usual dumps," she thought, kicking an empty Pop Tart box aside.

"Now remember all I told you," she said, loosening her grip on the small hand inside her own, no longer knowing whose sweat was whose, a gritty slipperiness that bound them.

She thought of Ned, on top — the stars sprayed out behind his head, neon-beaded sweat, his eyes jumping like a juke box — of how she rippled inside, and of the room where he trapped stars in his hammock, showed her Orion's glittering belt, the bear, the bird of paradise. "Like sparkling seeds," she thought, or something alive that she could feel expanding, a cluster beating far away, talking drums, heartbeat of the night. An easy coolness sliding between layers of heat, "Black Magic Woman" unwinding from the stereo into the stars; then his arms all around, containing her like no one ever had.

"Cassiopeia. That's a pretty name. Hey, you are what I want to be," he'd said that first night. "A star." Later, she felt his eyes touching her, but when she began to talk, they would slide off to the side and away. Even then she could see that his eyes were always working the crowd. She'd really known all along that he was a charming dead end, but he could say what she wanted to hear. She'd thought herself invulnerable to guys like him, especially guys who stood on a bandstand and sent it out to "all the real fine chicks, looking SO GOOD out there!"

A million "if onlys" later, she married him, against everyone's better judgment, determined to prove them all wrong, determined to beat the odds. But Ned wasn't playing the same odds. Ned always took the path of least resistance, and when things got rough after Hope came, he just cut loose. Very simple really.

And Cassiopeia just did what she had to do, what women alone with a child have always done: she got by. She found the cheapest grocery store in Bakersfield, a warehouse really, where she loaded Pablum, milk, canned goods onto huge dollies all by herself. She cocktailed and accepted checks from her mother from time to time. And she gave up the notion of ever getting a penny from Ned, who was by then falling off the bandstand every night by midnight.

* * *

She had the reddest blue eyes Cassiopeia had ever seen, a small chicken bone of a girl with strings of hair the color of tobacco juice and *Mothers Fucking Forever* tattooed on her forearm. "Chop Suey, get your butt in here," she snapped as the cat rivaling her for scrawniness shot through the crack of the door.

"Sorry about the cat," Cassiopeia began. The girl just stared.

"Hey, since when do you guys take kids out on a drop?" The girl's eyes lifted to a gray Riviera primed with clouds of metallic silver that had just pulled up to the curb. Cassiopeia could hear the thump of a bass behind the smoked-glass windows. The girl left, then reappeared with a wad of bills, just as the Riviera peeled off. "Who the shit ARE you?" The girl was now glaring at Cassiopeia, her blue eyes popping like firecrackers.

"I'm looking for Ned Quinlan." It seemed important to get on with her business and not mince around. And Cassiopeia wanted to get Hope out of there.

"I can't help you," the girl said. Chop Suey reappeared then with something shiny and black poking from his mouth. "Oh shit, another roach — SHOO — go on you disgustin' little creep!"

Then Cassiopeia saw. It was a huge cockroach the cat was delivering as trophy and gift. The girl lifted Chop Suey expertly with her toe and flipped her into the air and off the porch. Chop Suey's skinny spine whipped like a snake's as she skittered off, cockroach intact.

The girl sucked on a cigarette-stained tooth. "Look here, this ain't a good day for me, 'specially now.

Ned took off last week. Don't know where he is . . . Don't care."

"We're staying at the Capri Motel on Blackstone for now," Cassiopeia said, feeling the girl's itchiness to close the door. "I don't want money, didn't figure Ned to have any. I just want to talk to him, about something — important," she added.

"This Ned's kid?"

"Uh huh. This is Hope," smiling down at the child, who jumped at the sudden attention. When Cassiopeia looked up, the door was shut, "Another Tequila Sunrise" blasting out from behind the door's warped and blank face. Quickly Cassiopeia pulled Hope off the porch with her and half dragged her down the five blocks to the bus stop.

"Do I get a jet pop?" was all Hope could say as they waited in the broiling sun.

"Sure you do, honey. " Cassiopeia multiplied and subtracted numbers in her head. Like her mother, Eileen, Cassiopeia could perform feats of acrobatic equations in her head when it came to money, although she'd flunked algebra twice in high school. Cassiopeia sighed, decided she'd have to go looking for a job the next day. Her money was almost gone. She hadn't planned on it taking so long to find Ned. She'd have to take Hope with her, or find a playground with a kid's pool, a discovery she'd made in Bakersfield when she'd been cocktailing at The Blue Grasshopper. She'd get up in the mornings for breakfast with Hope and then, afternoons, they'd walk to a nearby park with a kiddie pool and lifeguard posted from one to four. She'd deposit Hope in the pool with orders not to budge until she came back. Then Cassiopeia would either nap or meet a customer for drinks.

A string of assorted losers and failed flirtations followed, until Hap Harvey had asked her to marry him the first time they'd slid into the red Naugahyde booth together. Hap had enough money to short out her mental calculator for good, but he also had a wife. But then, she had a husband, as the note Ned left had said, "in Fresno getting the Lovesick Cowboys back together." All she had when she took off for Fresno were a few scarred suitcases, Hope, and Hap's half-drunken promise to divorce his wife as soon as Cassiopeia got her own divorce. From the Amtrack window she'd watched Hap, all paunchy shine, growing smaller as the train pulled away, and she'd allowed the first tears to slide from a spring she'd thought had been dammed up inside of her at least twenty years before.

* * *

She was ten years old and had been kept out of school with the Asian flu for two weeks. The medicine was too strong, and she sat alone in the window where sun spilled into motes of dust, aware of her own separateness, of something even larger — something faceless and endless and without even a name. She saw a dark house with many rooms and over the doors, the words LOSS, NEW BODY PARTS, OPERATIONS, BILLS, SEX, RESPONSIBILITIES. She saw herself at the front door, and all she could do was cry. She began crying one afternoon and cried steadily for two days. On the evening of the second day, she lay in bed, her flannel pajamas all twisted and clammy. Even sleep, that sweet disappearing act that always whisked her away as a child, had retreated to the shadows and would not peform its one simple trick. Her feet and fingers began to itch, a tightness squeezed her chest, a huge bear hug of panic. She sat up in bed and dug her nails deep into her palms, causing a dark amoeba of blood to spread on her pajama top. The fear rose higher, engulfing her like a high fever. And she did the one thing she had not done for years: she ran to her mama's bedroom. But Eileen was not there. Heart scrambling, Cassiopeia went in search and found her on the back porch, well into her second gin and tonic, laughing with Juanita. Cassiopeia let go then and fell into her mama's flowery lap, sobbing, "I dunno, I dunno," to all of her questions. They took her off the medicine and she did get well, but looking back, nothing had ever been the same.

* * *

It was not for missing Hap that she cried now. In fact, quite the opposite. Seeing him there, as the train pulled out, so old and worn and with his funny, crooked glasses, Cassiopeia was suddenly aware of where her thirty years had taken her, and also aware that even this thread of hope she was hanging from was a dream thread — and fraying at that. The tears stormed their way through then while the train slid on beneath her, quiet and cool. Wanting to divert Hope, Cassiopeia leaned into the child's warm hair and whispered, "Let's count V.W. s."

Chapter 2
Chevyville, Illinois

There must have been a shortage of pigment when God mixed the color for Eileen's eyes, just the faintest wash, like weak, green tea. Not helping matters any, Eileen had the habit of staring into the distance as if seeing into the past and future at the same time, each cancelling the other out.

Eileen was living in Chicago and working in a cookie factory when, at nineteen, she got pregnant with Cassiopeia. She had a fling with a soldier on leave and she never saw him again. She told the story that they had been married before he left, and the aunt who had raised her believed the story, mostly because she wanted to. But not everyone in Chevyville believed it, even though Juanita swore she'd known the missing husband. It didn't help matters that Eileen refused to talk about it and discouraged any mention of that time of her life.

Eileen was a woman who in one breath might say, "We got to watch our pennies now. No extras for awhile," and in the next, "Let's live it up for a change. We can't deny ourselves forever." She was a potluck of contradictions, making it hard to be her child. She was at one moment fun and laughing, the next, distant and cool. About once a year she had a massive temper tantrum and tore the house apart, knocking over lamps, throwing magazines and cushions, overturning furniture, but amazingly, seldom breaking anything. She could only get away with it when they had their own place, so the fits gradually became less frequent.

Cassiopeia had long ago lost track of their moves; a P.O. box in Chevyville about six inches square was their only home base. And there had been a succession of men, "temporary fathers" for Cassiopeia, interrupted with about the same number of jobs for Eileen. When things got really rough, they went "visiting," which Cassiopeia eventually came to know for what it was: begging. There were some relatives in Memphis, always good for a few months, some scattered friends. And there was always Juanita. "Skinny as a fence post and twice as mean," she had been described once. Juanita collected bones and bird skulls, lining them up along her windowsills for the sun to bleach them. Anyone who found a raccoon, cow, deer, or any kind of bird bone, would drop it off on Juanita's porch thinking, "The things some people like."

"Why you think I stay in this snake pit?" Juanita would say. "I got too much stuff to ever move . . . Yep, me and my bones are stuck right here."

No one seemed to know how Juanita got by, always crying "broke" and, at the same time, buying Bootles by the case, the only gin she'd touch. "Born to drink good gin and love bad men," Juanita would say, laughing her crazy, child's laugh. "These fine lips deserve fine sips." Then she'd roll her big, deeply set eyes.

Juanita's greatest claim to fame, however, was as a party crasher. It got so bad, no one ever actually invited her, figuring she'd show up anyway. There was no party Juanita did not smell out. She also crashed weddings and hospitals, once sneaking into the intensive care room of a friend who wasn't allowed visitors. "Have I got the tonic for you!" Juanita whispered, pulling out the mixings for her famous gin and tonics, including fresh cut limes.

But the most famous crash, the one that went down in hers and Eileen's histories, was when Juanita talked Eileen into crashing Russell Haycraft's funeral. Eileen had schemed on Russell in high school and dated him their senior year. She had often thought she might have married Russell, but he fixed that by eloping, out of the blue, with Mary Beth Winter.

"That little poop-faced Baptist robot," Juanita said to Eileen. "You were just too much for him, girl."

Russell and Mary Beth had six girls in six years, and then Russell fell over dead one day of an embolism.

"Russell always did do things spur of the moment," Juanita said. Eileen was back in town, "visiting, between jobs," she told Juanita, who just hooted. "Between jobs, girl, says there's another one lined up."

Juanita waited until that night when Cassiopeia was in bed and they'd both settled into a few of her tonics to tell Eileen about Russell. Eileen surprised even herself by bursting into tears. They'd talked all night then, of Russell and high school times, and worked up a real mean gin buzz by early morning.

"O.K. girl," Juanita had said, scratching a match to the pilot light on the stove so she could start the coffee. "I got an idea. We're going to that funeral this morning."

"Come on now, Juanita, Mary Beth'd shit in her Lollipops if I showed up there. You told me once that Lily Vale said she even cut my pictures out of all Russell's yearbooks."

"So, we'll go in disguise. I can do wonders with wigs and make-up." They woke up Cassiopeia and dressed her like a boy, stuffing her long braids into a blue baseball cap. Cassiopeia would later remember their black crepe dresses, all swishy and dabbed with Chantilly to mask the gin smell, and big black picture hats with veils, and the pillow stuffing for Eileen's skinny hips. Nothing was more fun than being with Juanita in the midst of a scheme.

"Here girl, have some boobs for a change," Juanita said as she tossed two balloons to Eileen. Then her wild loon's laugh when one of the balloon-boobs flopped out and floated up to the ceiling. "Eileen, can't you keep your boobs in? Look, it's floatin' round the room!" More giggles and shrieks, with Juanita chasing the fugitive boob, hopping stocking feet onto the bed, her veil flapping. Cassiopeia joined in, trampolining onto the peacock chenille bedspread in her too-big Converse sneakers.

Finally, all boobs and hips, and veils in place, they jumped into Juanita's Mercury and headed for the cemetery for the eleven o'clock burial service, having missed the service at the funeral home. Juanita pulled out her harmonica and drove with one hand. Eileen and Cassiopeia sang "Swing Low, Sweet Chariot" then "Swing Low, Sweet Mercury," then "Sweet Limosine," "Sweet Motorcycle," and "Sweet Ford Fairlane Station Wagon." When they pulled up in the cemetery, they had to take deep breaths to compose themselves.

There were folding chairs set up around the gravesite. Reverend Blanchard was winding down the eulogy, a self-aggrandizing speech highlighting his own personal role in the salvation of Russell's soul. A good portion of Chevyville had gathered, and the only seats left were a half dozen, set up at the last minute, directly across from Mary Beth and the six little girls in mourning. Eileen, greatly sobered by the occasion, now began sniffling. She sniffled even more when she looked across the grave at the Haycraft girls, each almost a duplicate of Russell,with dimpled chins and wide-spaced, front teeth. One of the girls began passing out yellow roses from a basket wrapped with black crepe.

Juanita noticed then that Lily Vale had slipped into the chair beside Eileen and was staring suspiciously at the three of them. Eileen, still struggling with her tears, reached to take a rose from Russell's oldest. Later, they figured it must have been a thorn accidentally left on the rose's stem that did it. In the midst of a new and stronger surge of sobbing, a loud "POP" could be heard by most everyone at the front. In horror, Eileen felt her left boob deflate and with even greater horror watched Lily Vale's face fill with recognition.

"The nerve!" she hissed at Eileen. "Of all the tacky nerve!"

Eileen was a mess of tears now, overcome with

grief and humiliation, and could only sit there wiping her nose and eyes and snuffling.

Juanita had heard Lily, though, and hissed back, "Slut! Loudmouth sow!"

Fast as a hornet, Lily pulled the hatpin out of her wide-brimmed hat and poked it into Eileen's right boob. That did it. Juanita, always protective of Eileen, flew at Lily then, screaming, "Leave her alone, you cretin!"

The two of them took to each other with their patent leather purses. Juanita's was the bigger purse, and did the most damage the fastest, ripping out a chunk of Lily's snug chignon and dropping her to her knees with pain. Lily lunged for Juanita's legs, ripping out a nice handful of nylon hose.

Cassiopeia, followed by Eileen, had run for the car by now, horrified and embarrassed. They watched from across the softly mown lawn and rows of plastic bouquets what seemed to be a wild, flailing dance, Juanita and Lily and Reverend Blanchard caught between. Someone signaled to the Chevyville High Band and the strains of "Amazing Grace" wobbled weakly over it all.

All the way home, Cassiopeia watched the landscape shimmy as curtains of heat rippled up from the road ahead. She imagined they were driving under water, traveling to a new city deep under the sea. There, the only language was that of huge, lip-synching creatures. She gathered sea mushrooms and twining, luminous fruit from the ocean floor. The car was her private diving bell, and this was her first descent, sinking so deep into the secret aquamarine that she never even heard Eileen and Juanita arguing, blaming each other for the fiasco at the cemetery. Then came a long stretch of silence, then laughing so long and so hard that Juanita almost ran off the road.

Chapter 3

•

Fresno, California

Cassiopeia walked the six blistering blocks from the bus stop to The Satellite Lounge, Hope dragging backwards at her every step. The door was painted black and sprinkled with glitter, *The Satellite Lounge* in silver, with a big, loopy L. Inside was invitingly cool and dark after the heat of the blinding sun. Their eyes gradually adjusted in the stale-cigarette, flocked-wallpaper plushness. They crossed the floor and slid into a high-backed booth.

"Would you please bring my little girl a Coke and tell me where to find the manager?" Cassiopeia asked the waitress who had come to take their order. Her eyes looked tired and kind, and she seemed to size up the situation immediately.

"Sure thing, hon. Leave this little shortcake to Zona. I'll fix her up pronto." Clicking her tongue and winking at Hope, Zona motioned Cassiopeia to follow her. "Don't let Bud give you no bull. He needs another girl pronto. Ruby walked off the early shift two days ago, and Bud's in the middle of a nasty divorce. Wife's takin' him to Lamoures'." She winked again and opened the door marked MANAGER, sweeping Cassiopeia inside.

Bud Hesparian, very short and dark and with a bad haircut, was dressed completely in white. He did not rise from the desk but offered a hairy hand and an eternally suspicious smile.

"I take it you're applying for the cocktail waitress position?" A spray of spit came out with his words.

"Yes," said Cassiopeia. "I'm interested."

"Sit down, Miss uh . . ."

"Quinlan. Cassiopeia Quinlan."

"Usta know some Quinlans once, over to Sanger, round there. Well driller, he was. Wife had, you know," he said as he moved his index finger in a corkscrew motion near his right ear, "trouble upstairs."

"I don't have any relatives around here. I've only been in Fresno a short while." Cassiopeia waited while Bud Hesparian fitted his fingertips together, pyramid style.

"Have a seat," he said, pointing to a plastic chair. "So, Miss Quinlan, do you have any experience waitressing? Could you tend bar?"

"No, I couldn't tend bar, but I was a cocktail waitress at the Blue Grasshopper in Bakersfield for almost five years."

"Any letters of reference?"

Cassiopeia shook her head. "No, but I can get them. It will just take a few phone calls."

"Hmmmm . . . this is a very busy place. Tell you what. I can put you on right away, tips only, couple a weeks, see if you work out."

"Thank you," Cassiopeia said, rising. "I think I better just keep looking."

Bud Hesparian didn't move. "You can leave your number with Zona. That's a damn good offer, if you change your mind . . ."

"Thank you," said Cassiopeia, shutting the door behind her.

Now that her eyes had adjusted, the Satellite's glitzy veneer had diminished. The dark wood revealed a scrolled fakeness, and the dimly-lighted Gothic chandeliers resembled undismantled bombs. The Five Satins cooed "In the Still of the Night."

In her red booth, Hope sat on a booster, laughing and blowing the wrappers off straws at Zona, who mugged and giggled.

"This little girl of yours is a doll. Where can I get one just like her?"

"Believe me, you wouldn't want to do business with that guy," said Cassiopeia, and they both laughed.

"Well, did you get the job?" Zona asked.

"He offered me tips only for a couple of weeks. said no. Maybe I should do it, though."

"No siree, don't you do it. That skunk's got tons a money, but he's so cheap he even cuts his own hair, Willie BoBo style. Some contraption he has with a mirror to see in back that he bought mail order. Listen, hon, you leave everything to Zona. I'll just tell everyone who comes in the job's filled and after a couple more days busting his butt, he'll beg you to take the job. But ask for six bucks an hour, two weeks vacation, and sick pay. That's fair to start. Give me your number. Can you last a couple more days?"

Cassiopeia wrote the number on a napkin imprinted with a picture of a skunk holding a cocktail and saying, "Buy me a drink or I'll put up a stink."

"I hope so. This is really kind of you. I do need a job right away. And thanks for watching Hope, too."

"She's a sweetie." Zona winked.

Three days later, Cassiopeia had still not found a job, the Satellite Lounge hadn't called, and Hope was refusing to go to the kiddie pool that afternoon. Cassiopeia just gave up and decided not to go out job hunting. She sat drying her just-polished toenails in a sunny window, watching the fat bird perched on the orange 76 Union globe spinning in dizzy circles. Hope, whiney and bored, plucked at a scab. Cassiopeia thought maybe she should call Hap at work to see if he was back from his business trip. She was reaching for the phone when it rang. It was Bud Hesparian offering her the job.

Cassiopeia could hear Roy Orbison and bar laughter, like surf in the background. A half hour later Zona called. "You shoulda seen Bud an hour ago. Talk about an Armenian basket case. He was the unhappiest man at the happy hour. So I gave him a little nudge in your direction."

"But why did you do all this for me? I'm a total stranger to you."

"Well, I been where you are. And I gotta admit, your kid got to me. I'm not kidding, she's really something. I think she kinda took to me, too."

"Oh, I could tell she did," said Cassiopeia. "Speaking of Hope, I'm going to have to find a babysitter real fast. Do you have any ideas where I could look?"

"Hmmm . . . Well, let me check with my neighbor. She used to do that. I'll let you know."

The next morning when Zona called back, she sounded excited. "Listen, my neighbor can't do it, but I have an idea. Why couldn't I watch Hope since we'll be working opposite shifts? You could bring her over at eleven, and I could take her to work at six, where we'd make the switch."

Cassiopeia did not hesitate too long in accepting, especially since she was feeling somewhat desperate. This was really a huge relief. Cassiopeia thought of calling Hap at work that day, but her horoscope said, "Pull inward now. Wait for opportunities to come knocking. You still have your ace in the hole."

Cassiopeia sat on the narrow wrought iron balcony, watching morning light circle the parking lot like a big, frisky dog, her fingers curled around a coffee mug, steam ribboning up. In the distance, she heard the crunch of garbage trucks like huge can openers unzipping the day. She wanted to cry, but all the moisture had been wrung out of her in yesterday's heat. Relief made room for dismay.

"Another cocktailing job. Another round . . ." she thought. "Serve up another round of nothing, dead end on the side with a twist of stagnation." She thought of Hap not as a man but as a plan, an emergency exit. Why did it all seem so empty and pointless, just her and Hope? It was a feeling of incompleteness, of inadequacy, an emptiness she would like to fill. But she couldn't even imagine what to fill it with, except perhaps a man.

"What's wrong with me?" she asked the plastic plants. She stood up and looked out over Blackstone Avenue, an infinity effect of Wendy's, Taco Bells, Burger Kings. Fast fish, fast burgers, fast pancakes, fast chickens — never fast enough to escape their fates — whirled into popping oil. Huge baskets of chicken, offered up to the sky to the gods of finger lickin' enterprise — a king-size anchor dropped by the god of bad taste — golden arches, like suspension bridges spanning the miracle mile of frozen fries and smilie faces not having a nice day now or ever — a plaster, golden palomino rearing up and gelded by price wars and mothers angry at all the wrong things — Jack, fallen from his mythical stalk into a street-size Styrofoam box, sentenced to bob through diesel fumes and smog into the next ice age, slinky neck and bulgy eyes popping up through ice at the darkening sun.

Cassiopeia watched two hookers in the parking lot with a trick, a man who might have stepped out of the hardware department at Sears for his coffee break. Yesterday she had watched a thin girl in suicidally tight jeans bunny hopping at the bus stop in noon heat across from the Blackstone Shopping Mall. The girl stuck four fingers, like quote marks, on top of her head, yelled, sang, or prayed to the passing cars. From the city bus, Cassiopeia watched the girl hopping her psychotic way down Blackstone. She wondered where people like that ended up. She wondered if people know when they no longer control their own minds and if they are aware of another force that takes over their destiny. Did the girl know she had handed over her power?

Hope wheezed soft baby snores from the queen-sized bed. Cassiopeia, watching her, thought, "This minute, there are crimes being committed everywhere."

Chapter 4

•

Willahoma, Mississippi

Cassiopeia sat beneath the trees on a diamond wheel quilt stitched by her great aunt, Tiny Tears lolling beside her, purie blue eyes holding a dwarf sun in each resinous pupil. Cassiopeia had just had her fifth birthday, and Tiny Tears had risen that day from a nest of white tissue under a big red bow and come into her arms, clicking her glassy doll's eyes open and closed at Cassiopeia's command. Already she had taken her place with a shoebox bed, a set of acorn cups, a big magnolia blossom hat, and the name of Mazie. The name was bestowed by Cassiopeia in a moment of inspired desperation, mostly because it was the name of her Sunday school teacher and rolled off her tongue most easily.

"Mazie is hungry," Cassiopeia said aloud to no one. She opened her box of animal cookies, selected a sprinting tiger, and pressed it against Mazie's petal lips. Cassiopeia scooped up crumbs and stuffed the rest in her own mouth, then ate an elephant and two more puffy animals of unknown species. Mazie was a baby doll, but obliged all of Cassiopeia's fancies. Today Mazie was Cassiopeia's Indian sister, kidnapped by outlaws and held captive in an Arabian cave. Cassiopeia mounted Dancer, her white palomino, and galloped in circles, tossing her braided mane. She whinnied, slapped her thighs, and rode harder. "I must find her before sundown, Dancer," she said to her horse. "I know Mazie's in trouble. My magic ring is turning purple. Giddyup, girl!"

Digging her heels into Dancer's flanks, Cassiopeia charged forward then caught her toe in a creeping tree root and flew through the air, landing on the packed earth in a slapping bellyflop. The sky went white and her breath rushed out in one obliterating gush. For that instant, earth and air crystallized, and she froze inside the shell of her own blankness, like the soul of a bird leaving its hollow white bones behind. Her first new breath was a gulping sob. She ran to the diamond quilt and lay down, listening to her breath come and go. She held Mazie close and put her ear next to Mazie's tiny plastic nose. Nearby, she heard her name being called over and over. "Cass-eeee, Cass-eee." It was her cousin, Stinky, calling her, and Cassiopeia grabbed Mazie and hid in the dug out space of a tall, burned stump.

Stinky was one of many second cousins whose nickname at first was a joke and then gradually stuck. Cassiopeia did not like him. He was short and fat, his face speckled with moles, and his butch haircut only showed his somewhat pointed head to more disadvantage. Worst of all, Stinky did not know how to play. Some days Cassiopeia would use him as her patsy.

She'd bait, trick, and boss him around, the bandit slave to her outlaw queen. But mostly he just bored her; he could never think up anything, and after awhile he just dragged that day's game down. He wasn't even fun to hide from, like now, never really looking just wandering listlessly back and forth calling her name.

When Stinky had finally gone, Cassiopeia and Mazie came out. "I don't like him," Mazie said.

"He's just an icky old boy," said Cassiopeia, "but we'll get to play with Becky Lee tomorrow, Mazie. We're going to a party in Memphis. A family reunion."

"I want a new dress to wear," said Mazie.

"O.K." Cassiopeia smoothed the doll's flimsy, manufactured dress. "We'll go shopping in the morning in Paris, France."

"Where the girls don't wear underpants," Mazie giggled.

Cassiopeia smacked her, grinning. "That's a bad girl, Mazie."

Eileen had Sundays and Mondays off. She was working at the Jade Moon Tea House, having gotten the job through her cousin, Vangie, who was friends with the bartender, Sammy Sam. Vangie and her husband, Grady, had become regulars at the piano bar of the Shanghai Room. They ordered Stingers and sang the old songs: "On Top of Old Smokey," "Deep In the Heart of Texas," and their favorite, "Shine on Harvest Moon," with Germaine Geoffry, who wore her hair in a French twist and donned a different strapless gown every night of the week.

Vangie worked as a secretary at Cinderella Realty, and Grady did seasonal work. "Trouble is, it's never the right season for Grady to work," Vangie would say. She saw her role with children as giver of adult wisdom, and told Cassiopeia, "Never marry a Southern man. There's none of 'em worth a blue fig. Can't hold jobs or their liquor."

It was certainly true of Grady, whose eyes were perpetual wall-to-wall red and who "couldn't hold a job if it jumped into his arms," as Vangie said.

The morning of the reunion, Cassiopeia peeked into Eileen's room. It was still early, and Eileen lay with one arm thrown over her eyes, as if shading her sleep. Her red satin dress with the black frogs down the side was curled like a silken cat asleep beside the bed. Now that she worked late, Eileen slept in during the mornings. Cassiopeia crept around, waiting and trying her best to "be still." The smells of fried pork and My Sin mingled in Eileen's clothes, leeched into the room and mixed with a yellowish-pink cast from the flamingo shades, creating an exotic intimacy that invited Cassiopeia in. She liked it best then, while Eileen slept, never scolding her for touching her things, the only sounds her immutable breath and the faint tinkle of the painted slivers of glass on the oriental wind chimes. A lantern with satin tassles swung over the nightstand, where two wooden dolls offered their constant lips. There was also a miniature geisha doll who spun into a diamond-shaped mirror in a black laquered box, overlooking Eileen's fake gemstones and gold-filled charms. To Cassiopeia it was a cache of precious gems to mine before Eileen awoke.

This morning the room was a rosy amphora that sealed Eileen away from the passage of time. Tired of waiting, Cassiopeia wandered into the kitchen where Vangie was patting out circles of dough on a floured board, chopping celery, peeling potatoes, and boiling eggs for the reunion. They were all going to load into Vangie and Grady's Ford station wagon for the drive to Angel's Grove, just outside of Memphis. Besides Cassiopeia and Stinky, Jimmie Sue's three little girls were going with them. They had been visiting since Jimmie Sue went in for her operation. Southern women were always going in for mysterious operations, the cause of which no one would say. There were four adults counting Uncle Arlie, who stayed in his back bedroom all day napping under the churn of an electric fan.

Cassiopeia ate biscuits soaked with butter and rhubarb jam then scooted out the back door with Mazie. She had her new tank suit under her sundress and had snipped off the cuff of one of Grady's socks for a swimsuit for Mazie. They were entering a bathing beauty contest, and she had also stolen ribbon and the satin sash of Vangie's dressing gown to fasten over their shoulders for their beauty titles. Under the shade of a sweet gum tree, she practiced announcing into a fountain pen microphone swiped from Eileen: "And here comes the lovely Mazie Blue from Willahoma, USA. Her talent, ladies and gentlemen, is contortion. Here she comes now." Cassiopeia had seen a newsreel in which a contortionist stood on her hands, pulled her legs under her torso, and balanced a cup of coffee on each foot. Mazie complied now, as far as her polyurethane legs would give, amazing Bingo, the cat, with her twisting and torqueing. Cassiopeia was just scribbling her child's version of MISS UNIVERSE on the sash with the fountain pen when she heard Eileen calling. Before she could stash everything away, Eileen was standing over her.

"When did you get my good pen, Little Miss? And what's that behind your back? Give it to me right now." Cassiopeia's small, doomed fists couldn't completely conceal the sash that fluttered out, bleeding violet ink. "Cassiopeia Lane! Why did you do this? You've ruined the belt to Vangie's robe."

Cassiopeia felt herself lifted by one arm, dangled like a caught fish. Then the blaze of a sweet gum switch set fire to her legs, striping them up and down. Later, lying on her soaked pillow, she didn't remember the switch's sting, the pain. She remembered only Eileen's words, sharp as barbed wire, and her face, bright red and twisted. To make matters even worse, Eileen informed her that she wasn't "dragging Mazie along" as she climbed over the station wagon tailgate, where the children had been herded. Then Stinky pressed his moist thigh against hers all the way to the reunion. His neck was ringed with rivulets of grime and sweat that collected in the folds.

Cassiopeia, who was now mad at the world, focused her disparate unhappiness onto his unknowing, pudgy self, digging her longest fingernail into the soft flesh under Stinky's thigh, leaving a white crescent moon scar. He had been dozing, his head close to Grady's snoring face against the back seat. Grady and Uncle Arlie had dropped off before they had passed the neighbor's mailbox. Startled from his sleep, Stinky yowled right into Grady's ear and got a good, hard blow from the equally startled Grady, neither one knowing what had happened.

They finally arrived in Angel's Grove, just outside of Memphis. They had taken over about a dozen long, stone tables that were quickly loaded down with fried chicken, potato salad, watermelons, peach pies, chess pies, homemade pickles, and pickled rhubarb. Cassiopeia felt herself swept up into enormous voile bosoms, surrounded by waves of rayon-smothered flesh. She was scooped up and examined for Davis traits — Eileen's family — and asked whom she favored. Everyone seemed to be a second or third cousin or half-something, once or twice removed. Cassiopeia was trying to escape the press and cloister of relatedness, when a shrunken man with no hair at all and age spots big as saucers blocked her path with his wheel chair.

"Look a here, mama. She looks just like 'er daddy. Yup, spittin' image a her papa."

Vangie, who stood nearby with Eileen, tried to shush him up, but the circle around him had grown suddenly still, and the old guy, senile past the point of being shushed, continued. "If I didn't know better, I'd think her papa was standin' right here before me."

Finally Vangie said, "That's right, she looks just like her papa," and grabbed up Cassiopeia's hand. "C'mon, Cassie. Let's go find Becky Lee."

Cassiopeia's father had long ago joined the ranks of taboo subjects: female problems, missing relations, questionable births, any mention of domestic troubles. If any of the talk that went around got back to Eileen she never let on.

It was very late when the empty bowls and

sleeping children were piled into the back end of the Ford. The reunion was already becoming a blur of smothering skirts, chigger bites, slow gossip, and paper fans. Wide awake, Cassiopeia squeezed into the back of the station wagon last and lay against the gate so she could see out the window. There was no moon, and the night sky was churning with stars. As it moved, the car seemed to be fixed while the great, sparkling wheel of the sky spun overhead. The night air smelled of a green river. Cassiopeia drew the river in with her breath, let it wash her away like a drop of water slung from a water wheel, a piece of the shine waxing and waning on the river's face. She closed her eyes.

Who were these people with her on this dark journey, these people who called her one of their own? Why was she connected to them at all? She thought of all the nameless skirts encircling her that day, the Desert Flower kisses she wanted to wipe away. They meant nothing to her. They were strangers who brushed against her, mispronounced her name, and unraveled the blood lines between them like some kind of family rebus. Vangie's sister's child, the one who has seizures, she's fourth cousin to Grady's mama . . .

Cassiopeia knew she had another name, a name that waited for her in a cold region distant and unknown, having nothing to do with this car and its people. And some day she would live there. She wanted to open the back end of the car and perch on the edge of the disappearing road, to climb up over the black trees they now passed between to a place where she could swim the ladder of dark rivers, untouched, numinous, and completely alone.

Chapter 5
•
Fresno, Calif.

At first the hotel had been exciting, like a movie star's palace. Hope loved the wide, fringed bed that shimmied for a quarter, the leopards wiggling their spots overhead, the sweet candy smells of disinfectant, and their drinking cups, wrapped in cellophane. But there was no swimming pool and no other children for miles. There didn't seem to be any children at all in this new town. But then Hope saw a few on the bus and a lot more later at the playground pool. She was always glad to see them, the way adults are always glad to recognize their own kind in a foreign country.

This was like being on vacation all the time — until her mother started dragging her to playgrounds and on and off buses again. And it was so stinking hot her K-Mart underwear stuck to her bottom when she stood up. Cassiopeia bought her a pair of sunglasses with swans on the rims, and she wore them everywhere. She had her stuffed dolphin, too. But there was so much that was new and so many scary people, like the old man who shuffled by the motel every morning in his bedroom slippers, suitcoat and red baseball cap flipping cigarette butts over his shoulder. The sunken spot where his mouth should be scared her, but he never even looked her way. It seemed to Hope that she was either gushed over or ignored by adults.

But she did like Zona. And why not? Zona thought Hope was better than the baby Jesus. Hope had only to blink an eye and Zona would applaud. Every day now they made a plan. They popped popcorn and watched soaps together, Zona hollering, "Leave that bastard, you fool" and then to Hope, "I don't know why Erica stays with Mallory. He's nothing but trouble."

They built a playhouse for Hope out of cardboard boxes they discovered behind Thrift City, where Zona bought old curtains and rugs for the inside. Hope took markers and drew windows and wallpaper on the sides of the box. All of one week, Zona let Hope take her lunch into the cool recesses of cardboard. One afternoon they filled Hope's wading pool with soapy water and carried all the knick-knacks out to the backyard. Hope climbed into the pool with a sponge, and Zona launched knick-knacks to her: little ceramic skunks with *The Satellite Lounge* painted in gold on their tummys; a whole zoo of ceramic animals, including a snake and an armadillo stamped with Waco, Texas. There were Eiffel Tower salt and pepper shakers, a little Dutch girl and boy, and a ballerina on pointe. Hope was very careful, but somehow the ballerina's dainty index finger got broken. They discovered it while Zona was testing Hope's memory of where each knick-knack belonged. Hope felt the big, guilty tears collecting weight enough to coast downwards, but Zona, recognizing that look, just laughed.

"You know what, Hopie? This ballerina belonged to my Aunt Tina Marie, who broke that very same finger once when she got it stuck in between two metal bars on the Coney Island ferris wheel. Imagine that. Now its just perfect." Hope believed the story, because who would make up a thing like that?

They dressed in fine dresses and sat at Zona's redwood picnic table, serving high tea to the Queen. Zona pulled out the Queen's chair and then curtsied. "That dress is divine, your highness. Care for a crumpet?"

Hope fell into this foolishness easily. "Does the King like jelly doughnuts?" This sent Zona off into rolls of laughter that brought her to tears.

One morning when Cassiopeia dropped Hope off, Zona was all excited, packing up a lunch of cold, leftover mashed potatoes, pizza, and Cokes. "No reason we have to eat boring old sandwiches just cuz we're packing a lunch." When Hope asked where they were going, Zona just winked. "Surprise" was all she'd say.

Hope stuck her head out the window of Zona's car, letting the wind slap against her tongue as they passed the parking lots of K-Mart, Pep Boys, McDonald's, and Caeser's Golden Horse on their way out of town. Asphalt and concrete simmered, the air so dry and hot that "breathing it in could burn your lungs," according to Zona.

They turned off the highway and drove along a gravel road until they came to a tall, chain link fence and a big sign that said Rice Road Dump. Zona parked the car and told Hope to stay put while she talked to the man. She talked a long time. At first they seemed to be arguing, and then they laughed. She got back in then, and they waited while the old guy took the padlock off the gate and motioned them through.

"Your mama ever buy you blackberries?" Zona asked Hope, who shook her head "No" as they crunched along slowly past tall mountains of trash, mournful chairs, rusted cribs, stained mattresses with uncurled springs, and more — articles jumbled or weathered beyond recognition. Hope saw a gutted doll's house with just the painted-on shrubbery and stairs left on the peeling, blackened shell.

They parked the car again, and Zona pulled two metal buckets out of the trunk. They walked, Hope pinching her nose closed at the mouldering smells of damp garbage and burnt tires. They passed through a gate and into another section where shells of rusting cars were stacked up like giant squashed cans.

"It's a car graveyard. But if you look closely", Zona said, pointing to a hoodless Datsun against the fence, "it's a blackberry patch."

Zona pulled some sticky vines up from under a tire and showed Hope a cluster of thick, dark berries. Plucking carefully, she dropped them with a firm "thunk" into her bucket. She handed the other bucket to Hope. Hope took the metal handle and looked around. She reached under a fender among the brambles and found another dark cluster, then pulled back quickly from the sharp sting.

"Careful, baby, they bite," said Zona, showing her

how to lift the vines with a stick, and then carefully pull the plump berries loose. Hope had only covered the bottom of her bucket when they found the muddy green Ford Pinto with all four doors drooping open and the interior a sprawling mass of prickly vines. Zona sat in the cracked vinyl driver's seat picking berries from under the dash. Hope's palms deepened to a rich purple; blue seeped under her nails. Their buckets filled with berries — small, dark bodies, warm and almost breathing.

They rested, leaning into the Pinto's shade. Hope popped one berry into her mouth, let it melt there, sweet-tender, a purple juice running down onto her chin. She closed her eyes. The sun swam overhead, heat splashing down onto the roofs of baking cars. She could hear the fizz of bluebottle flies, a tractor's lazy drone.

"Hush little baby, don't you cry, Mama's gonna bake you a blackberry pie. And· if that berry pie ain't sweet, Mama's gonna buy you a diamond ring." Zona's voice was fading. "Next week . . ." she said.

But Hope didn't hear any more as she slid into a warm, metallic sleep. Next week the cars would still be there, corroding in their mass grave, the berries ripening under bald tires and dead transmissions. But Hope would be far away, crisscrossing the path of the sun, and Zona would be locked away, spitting at sterile, white, unanswering walls.

Chapter 6
•
Chevyville, Illinois

She kept forgetting to call him Dad. Mostly she just felt too embarrassed although she wasn't even sure why. But worst of all, Eileen wanted her to use his last name. They had both been using the name Lane, Eileen's supposed married name. And now, Cassiopeia Applegarth. It sounded stupid. She just couldn't do it. But Eileen had been to three conferences with her teacher, and they'd all sat down and discussed it, which meant that Eileen and Red had tried to "reason" with her. Cassiopeia couldn't think of anything to say. It was a stupid name, and she didn't see why she had to use it now just because "they" were married. But when they asked her why, she just shrugged and picked at the peeling rubber of her sneaker. Finally, she said, "I can't spell it." So Eileen fixed that, bought an ID bracelet, and had her name engraved on it, C. *Applegarth*, and she was made to wear it to school every day. Unable to think of any more excuses, Cassiopeia was stuck now with the name and the bracelet.

Juanita said that either Red Applegarth's mother had been guided by a gypsy, or he had grown to suit his name. He was big as a tree with pale, reddish hair and complexion, and looked as if he'd always just come in out of the sun. He had a jutting jaw and freckles even on his lips and up inside his nose. Cassiopeia knew because she had looked one day when he slept on his back under the chestnut tree, his mouth open to the sky. Red was building her and Eileen a house.

Eileen would make peanut butter sandwiches, and they'd drive out to the old Blankenship place to tear it down for the two-by-fours and usable lumber. Eileen pulled nails, and Cassiopeia helped until she got tired and started "acting up." Then Eileen would shoo her away to color or explore. Cassiopeia loved poking into the rubble of the rooms, opening old cupboards, stepping on the pedal of the rusted garbage pail, hearing the slurp of the lid. In the kitchen she discovered a door that opened to a dark pantry tucked under stairs leading up to what Cassiopeia imagined as the devil's hideout. The stairs seemed to lead straight up and disappeared in an old perfumey blackness as deep and treacherous as all her fears. Cassiopeia fumbled up four steps and felt a rush of stale air, a brush against her leg, feathery, wild, and warm. Every muscle jumped, and her heart flipped like a docked fish.

The next day she couldn't wait to go back. This time, she stayed in the pantry long enough for her eyes to adjust and found an old, tin cookie box filled with shiny buttons, garters, a crumbly envelope with coils of colorless hair folded over softly inside, and a bottle of Blue Waltz perfume with a violin and roses on the label. The box smelled of a sick kind of sweetness, a place from the past, and gave her a queer feeling like when she ate too much cake. But she opened it again and again with an irresistible acquiescence.

Red began work on the new house in June. They tossed in one of Cassiopeia's baby shoes, a scarf of Eileen's, and an Ace of Diamonds for luck as the foundation was poured. Cassiopeia watched her shoe sucked under the creamy concrete while Red and Eileen spread and smoothed.

They all scratched their initials into the front porch. Mornings were hammered and pounded open now, Red's band saw zinging into the noon hour. Cassiopeia sifted through sawdust for nickle-sized plugs, filled her change purse with them, and danced in the shaved wood curls through the tall cage of their future home, giving the rooms the names of the rooms in her Clue game: the billiard room, the library, the conservatory.

At night, Red smoked cigars and played cards, mostly solitaire, or his favorite, hearts, if he could find players. Sometimes Juanita would bring over Mick and Nick Laird, her twin nephews, whose specialty was horseplay. Rick winked at Cassiopeia and called her beautiful, his words smooth as the Vitalis he used to slick back his hair. Juanita, Eileen, and Cassiopeia would go off to see movies, with titles like *Honky Tonk*, *Robber's Roost*, and *Not as a Stranger.*

All the way home, and weeks later, Cassiopeia would be lost in her private soundtrack. Under the movie's spell, she imagined what Debbie Reynolds or Deborah Kerr would do or think or say. It was with their words that she answered Red or Eileen or the man at the store. And if the movie was a murder mystery, she would be sure the postman was really a killer, hiding bodies in his truck under the mail bags. She plotted elaborate schemes to trap him, leaving a note in a neighbor's box that said, "If you did it, you won't go to the water tower tonight." At the water tower she'd leave another note saying, "I knew it was you. Now you are going to pay."

Eileen had definite ideas of how she wanted things done, and Red just about never got it right. If he watched football on a Sunday afternoon, he was "always hanging around" making her nervous. If he went fishing, he was "never at home."

"Sugar, where do you want this hose put?" he'd ask. "Do I have to tell you where every little thing goes?" she'd say.

But sure as he put it somewhere on his own, it was, "Oh Red, no, not there. Not right where I'm trying to get the ivy to spread."

But Red was crazy about Eileen, and it seemed that the sheer bulk of him absorbed all her insults, her picky complaints and nagging. Red would just widen his apple-faced grin, his eyes tucked away in slits of laughter.

Eileen had the habit of disappearing into the bathroom for hours. It was an unsolved mystery what she did in there, and Red never tired of asking. And then, shaking his head, he'd chuckle. "You could have learned to speak Greek in there by now, Eileen." Eileen completely ignored all this, and as to what she did in there, she never volunteered a clue. Once Red even timed her. "Exactly fifty-three minutes," he crowed, and he would have made a routine of it if Eileen hadn't said she'd go use the restroom down at the Standard Station from now on if he didn't stop.

Eileen and Red had met at the dentist's office when Cassiopeia was having a check-up. The three of them were the only patients in the waiting room for over an hour before discovering that Dr. Ramsey, who was getting on in years, had confused his schedule and left early. His nurse was ill, and he just forgot to check the waiting room and left by the side door, locking them inside. Red had to pick the lock into the nurse's station to get to a telephone and call poor Dr. Ramsey, who was full of embarrassed apologies. But Eileen and Red just laughed, thought it was the funniest thing, and made a date to go to the movies.

Red was new in town and Juanita would later say that she had always been suspicious of him, although no one really remembered her saying so at the time. In fact, she was the one who married them. They'd all been on a picnic and were driving back late, Eileen and Red in the back seat, Cassiopeia and Juanita up front. Suddenly, out of the blue, Red said, "Eileen, sweetie. If you'll marry me, I'll build you a brand new house."

"All right. When?" Eileen said.

"Right now," Red replied.

And Eileen said, "Stop the car."

Juanita had a mail-order minister's license she'd only used once before, and she pulled over right in the middle of a field. Rows of corn, like fluted columns, rose up around them. The moon was riding high and full, dissolving in and out of the faint clouds. Cassiopeia sunk sleepily into soft clods of dirt. The night winds batted the streaming tassles, set them to whispering and rustling their silk. Everyone was a little drunk, even Cassiopeia who was still whoozy with sleep and the rocking of the car.

It was a night for ritual without words, and no one would remember later what was said. But they'd all remember the big, bulging moon and how the corn-fields crashed upwards to the black sky like huge waves parting just for them.

Red had money from his last job, he said, in Kansas City, where he had worked in a planing mill. "Foreman," he said, "paid real well." He hinted at other sources of income too, but gave no details and never really explained why he had left.

Red wore a pith helmet and canvas apron of tools. He could lift the beams for the outside walls of the house by himself with his wide, freckled shoulders. Cassiopeia thought of Paul Bunyan when she watched him on the roof pounding shingles, his head eclipsing the sun. He called in a plumber and electrician but did everything else himself, climbing up ladders with bundles of shingles, hauling bricks and wheelbarrows full of cement. And gradually the house took shape, just as inside Cassiopeia something began to take shape, a picture of herself as occupant with all the privileges that brought: a key on a rabbit's foot keychain, friends coming home with her after school, showing them around the house. "And this is the L-shaped living room, and here, a breeze-way, my room . . ."

She lay down on the fresh plywood where her bed might go, watching puffs of clouds foam through beams that rose up like the walls of a huge crib. There had always been something missing in her life, but the curious thing was that the "not having" denied knowl-edge of anything else. How could she know what was missing if it had never been there? Its presence was defined by its absence. It was like driving by houses at dusk, the pinkish amber color of the sky superimposed upon blackening windows. It was the unsettling knowl-edge of something unknowable, like imagining death. And in her instinctual drive to imagine what it was that was missing, she endowed it with such power and magic that reality would always be for her a crash land-ing, the jerk of the kite string that brought her reluctant-ly back to earth.

They were two weeks away from moving into the house. It was a night of clinging heat. Even the walls were sticky. Eileen was watching t.v.; Red had disap-peared into the bedroom. They had just gotten back from a fish fry about twenty miles north. Juanita had driven and was speeding, as usual, when they heard a siren behind them. The state patrolman had been very nosy, asking all kinds of questions. He even asked to see Eileen and Red's I.D.s. Juanita thought the cop "was really nervy." When she dropped them off, she was still complaining about him.

Cassiopeia heard canned laughter in the living room. She was lying on her sleeping bag, having tem-porarily moved onto the back porch when Red moved in. She watched the fitful blinking of fireflies outside in the cool grass. On her way into the kitchen, she passed Eileen and Red's room and stopped suddenly, not knowing why.

Red had an open suitcase on the bed. He saw her, too, and for an instant they both froze. Then he just continued folding his clothes into the suitcase. His calmness made Cassiopeia wonder if she should say something. Maybe Eileen knew about this. They were always making plans without telling her. She passed the front room where Eileen lounged in one of Red's huge t-shirts. Cassiopeia poured out a glass of chocolate milk. She called for Eileen, but Eileen wasn't budging.

"No, you come here," Eileen called back. Before Cassiopeia could answer, she heard a heavy knocking at the door.

"Police. Open up right now." Eileen had pulled on a pair of jeans, and opened the door to two looming policemen.

"Can we speak to Jack Applegarth?" the taller of the two said, without wasting any time. They both seemed jumpy and very grim. Eileen called for Red, but no answer came from the bedroom.

Cassiopeia came out then from the kitchen and said, "Mama, I was trying to tell you. I saw Red filling his suitcase . . ."

"You get the front door, I'll get the back." They were running now through the small house, and the tall one knocked over a lamp on his way to the back door.

"What's going on here?" Eileen demanded, but they were both lunging out the doors. Cassiopeia could hear staticy voices from a short wave radio in the darkness and could see the beams of flashlights twirling over their tiny, rented yard. Then the cops' voices: "O.K., you get on the radio, Pete."

"Yea. Looks like he gave us the slip."

Eileen told Cassiopeia to sit on the sofa and not to move and went outside with the cops. Cassiopeia could catch only a few words now and then. When Eileen came in, the cops behind her, her face was drained of its color and she had the stiff look she got before one of her fits.

The cops questioned Cassiopeia, scaring her with their sharp questions. Did Jack say anything to her? Did she know where he was going? Was she telling the truth?

They searched the house then, pulling out the sofa, looking places Red couldn't possibly have fit. Eileen sat on the sofa, looking ill. Cassiopeia wanted to ask her questions but was too embarrassed, and Eileen had her Ice Queen mask on anyway, the "look that would stop the devil in his tracks," Red liked to say.

But Cassiopeia was used to not being told what was happening. Most of what she came to know was through overheard conversations or a confused sort of sixth sense that children in households such as hers develop. They become unwilling private eyes, able to decipher any code with the sketchiest of clues and knowing the truth at some foggy level beneath consciousness.

Cassiopeia did not find out what happened until the next day when she overheard Eileen on the telephone with Juanita.

"God, Juanita, it was a nightmare. You should have seen us. They stormed in here and searched the house just like we were common criminals . . . Well, yea, I guess he is. He's wanted in Kansas City for bank robbery. Can you believe it? Very funny, Juanita. How can you make jokes? I didn't sleep at all last night . . . They have a warrant out for him. And that's not the worst of it. Oh, so you heard . . . That's bigamy, Juanita. Well, to be honest, mÿ nerves are shot . . ."

Going to Juanita's was the natural thing to do. It had always been a sanctuary for them. Eileen said she wasn't afraid of Red, but she felt better out of the house anyway. Several weeks later they heard he was in jail in Davenport, Iowa. Eileen stuffed all that was left of Red into the trash, the stretched out t-shirt she was wearing the night he ran away, a cigar box full of orphaned keys, and a rattley tackle box with a tangle of lines and mud-caked lures, emblems of the mystery he had now become in her mind and could never have been in reality: a man possessed of a most routine and conventional nature. Eileen never knew if Red had tried to call the old house. She felt completely betrayed by his running away without so much as a word to her and by the knowledge of his other wife, which voided his marriage to her. She had been so caught up in the new house, she had never really reflected on her feelings for Red. But reflections were pretty much foreign to her anyway.

Juanita treated the situation somewhat lightly, cracking jokes about Red's last job being a profitable one, for sure, and she didn't think "getting married in a cornfield" was legal anyway. She referred to the house as Red's hideout. When it was confiscated by the bank's lawyers, even Juanita was surprised at Eileen's coolness. And when she wanted to drive over for one last look, Juanita protested, but took her anyway. Cassiopeia had gone with them at the last minute, but wouldn't get out of the car when they pulled up in front. She sat, twisting her foot in the rope swagged across the back of the Chevy's front seat.

She thought of her shoe, Eileen's head scarf, and Red's card, sunken forever in their cement tomb. She thought of the coil of lost hair she'd found in the cookie box. She thought of that movie where the greedy Egyptian king was trapped in the tomb as it sealed around him, one passageway after another filling with sand. She felt a numb kind of sadness but not for the lost house. Her daydreams had many houses and many rooms. And not for Red; she was glad he was gone. Now she didn't have to say Cassiopeia Applegarth, and she got a larger piece of the slim piece of the pie that was Eileen's attention.

"My dad's in jail," she said out loud, but didn't know if she believed it. It was the first time she'd called him Dad. The only things Eileen had told her directly were "Don't worry about any of this. He's not your real Dad anyway," and "The marriage has been annulled, so it's best if we just forget all about it." When Cassiopeia asked what annulled meant, however, Eileen said, "It means we were never married at all."

Cassiopeia looked startled. "But Mom, I was there, how can . . ."

"Look," Eileen said, "the law says it didn't happen. So that's the end of that." Her face got all crumbly looking.

But Cassiopeia persisted, "How can something not happen that did?"

"You'll understand someday."

But when Cassiopeia saw the hard shine of tears in Eileen's eyes, she was more confused and didn't think she ever would understand.

But if Cassiopeia didn't miss Red, she missed something, something without a name, an idea maybe, perhaps containing the three of them, or a state of being played slow motion with blurred background and piano crescendo on the soundtrack. The missing part was what no one would ever see, a strip of celluloid spliced out and tossed away. And her sadness felt the same as what she felt when the little girl's movie mother died. But that was a sadness peculiar to children, lasting not much longer than the popcorn or the newsreel, and it really belonged to someone else and, thus, was easily dispelled in the distance between dark theatre and piercing daylight. This was different.

As they pulled away from the house Eileen would never decorate and Cassiopeia would never show off to the friends she'd never have, the sun burst fiery and finite in the rear-view mirror, exploding the street and all else that narrowed behind them. Before they had passed the end of the block, Cassiopeia was begging for a dairy delight, and Juanita was saying, "O.K., if you'll watch for cops so I don't get another ticket. We got enough trouble with the law already."

Chapter 7
·
Fresno, California

The Hamm's waterfall dripped its reflection into veined mirrors behind the Satellite Lounge bar. The waterfall came from the old Moon Dog Inn. Bud got it for thirty dollars at the swap meet where he took his girlfriend, Yolanda, when Betsy, his wife, went off to have her acrylic nails wrapped. Zona had once said maybe Bud and Betsy would have made it if Betsy had spent as much time with Bud as she did with her manicurist.

It was a slow day, a few regulars at the bar, a young couple melted together in a booth, lost in each other. Twin t.v.s flipped through mute commercials, liar's dice and laughter mingling for sound. Cassiopeia didn't know if she was more bored or tired, but she did know that her feet hurt. The clock seemed frozen at five-thirty. She refilled white, ceramic cubes with sugar packets and dumped ashtrays until five-forty nine. Marie, the bartender, laid down an iced Coke for her. "Take a load off, kid."

Cassiopeia sat down at the bar, turning the

pages of a creased *Glamour* magazine. "Look at those hats," Roger, the carpenter said. "Looks like coneheads are making a comeback."

"That's high fashion, Roger," said Marie, who moved from the taps to the cash register with the fluidity of a sleek seal.

"Hand Jive" jumped from the jukebox. Cassiopeia looked up and waved to Bill at the end of the bar, who had just played her favorite. When six o'clock came, Cassiopeia got her purse. Zona, who usually got there a few minutes early, was late. When Zona finally arrived she was loaded down with several shopping bags. Cassiopeia noticed something was different about her, but she wasn't sure just what, something about her gestures, like pinballs bouncing off flippers. Her eyes shone with a feverish light.

"Sorry, sorry, sorry," Zona said. "Apologies all around. Set 'em up, Marie. Apologies for everyone!" She waved her hand expansively. Hope sat down in a booth and laid her head heavily on the counter. "This little shortcake's all tuckered out. Can't keep up with old Zona."

"Is everything all right?" asked Cassiopeia, feeling an unspecific sense of alarm.

"Oh sure, honey. Me and Shortcake went shopping. You should see what we bought."

Zona pulled out three sweaters, identical except that they were three different pastel colors, out of a huge black and gold shopping bag. "Pure cashmere, baby doll. And look at this lipstick. What do you think of this peach shade on me? Iced Sherbert," she said from between smooched lips, leaning into the bar mirror and smearing lipstick with a frantic finger. She pulled out a lizard handbag, a frothy pink camisole, two watches that were, she said, "a damn steal, just couldn't pass 'em up." More bottles and tubes of cosmetics emerged, a wrist-full of clanky bracelets, and a purple straw hat shaped like an oversized frisbee.

She accompanied this boisterous show and tell with a frenzied patter, the words spilling over each other. She called to Hope to "come show off your things, Shortcake." But Hope couldn't lift her head from the oval of her arms, her eyes rolling sleepily.

"I better get her home," said Cassiopeia, almost having to carry Hope out of the bar. The last she saw, Marie was helping to stuff things back in the shopping bag and at the same time trying to put a lid on Zona, whose laughter burst out in progressive flurries, trailing them into the parking lot and all the way down to the crosswalk. Hope, so exhausted she could hardly walk, barely hauled herself to the bus stop. She slept all the way to the motel, her face a dimpled design where it had flattened against the side of the bus. Cassiopeia asked her over their chili dog dinner at Der Wiener Schnitzel where she had gone that day with Zona.

"Lots of stores," she said. "We bought a lot of things, Mommy. Zona kept saying we'd just go to one more. Did you see what she got me? I picked it all out by myself." Cassiopeia had opened Hope's bag on the bus and found four sunsuits, a ruffled blue swimsuit with spouting whales, a raccoon squeeze toy, two coloring books, and a straw visor with a green, see-through bill. "We used our credit cards!" Hope chirped proudly. Cassiopeia felt a worried kind of irritation and found this last statement especially annoying.

"They are HER credit cards, Hope, not ours. And I think that was a very foolish thing to do. Zona will still have to pay for all this," she snapped, causing Hope's smile to crumble.

That night Hope fell asleep over her Flintstone coloring book, the fat, purple crayon with which she had given Bam Bam purple eyeballs gripped in her hand. Cassiopeia carried her, wrapped in a cream-heavy obliteration, her eyelids translucent as bird throats, to the queen-sized bed. "Lost to the world," she thought. "I'll never sleep like that again in my life." Hope's spindly arms and legs angled off in all directions as Cassiopeia tucked her in.

It was close to midnight when the phone rang. Cassiopeia jerked up and lunged for it. It was Marie at the Satellite. "Cassie, I just thought I should call you. For one thing, I figured this will affect you too. They've taken Zona away."

"Who? Who took her?"

"Well, first it was the cops. Cassie, I've never seen her like that. She started talking crazy, reading palms, telling jokes. I couldn't even get her to wait on customers. She wanted to call out for Chinese food, and she was throwing ice at Bill — they got in a big ice fight. It was like having some teenager running amuck. Then she propositioned some old guy coming out of the can. Wouldn't let him pass by her. She just got real stubborn. I couldn't get her to budge. I called Paul to come in and relieve me so I could drive her home, but before he got here, she ran out in the parking lot, stripped off half her clothes, and lay down right there in front of a car singing "Onward Christian Soldiers." Cassie, it was awful to see her like that. I found a number for her sister on her application in Bud's office. The sister lives in the mountains and said she'd come down but meantime somebody'd called the cops. When they came, she just got real mean, spitting at them, calling them Nazis. She fought the two of them. Big guys, too. She put up a good fight, but they wrestled her into the car and took her off screaming. Thank God it was slow. Not that many customers saw it all. When her sister showed up, she told me that she'd see to getting Zona put in the hospital again. Seems this has happened before. Said she must have gone off her medication, and right when she was doing good, too. She's O.K. if she'll just take it, the sister said."

"What's it for?" Cassiopeia asked.

"Sister said it was for manic depression, I think. Yea, that's it. I guess that's what all that shopping was about. I thought that was pretty weird. Poor Zona."

"Yes, poor Zona," said Cassiopeia, feeing guilty for immediately thinking of her own situation. Now she had no one to watch Hope. She hung up the phone and sat in darkness, looking out over the empty motel parking lot, the traffic winding out on Blackstone. "I've got two days off to figure out what to do now." Her immediate dilemma dulled her sympathies for Zona. "I should have known this was too good to be true."

Cassiopeia slept fitfully that night and woke at five-thirty, her lower back speared with pain. Then she remembered what her uneasy sleep had blotted out. "Oh God, Zona." Cassiopeia got up and sat in her nightgown beside the window watching the morning sky give up its darkest edges to a pink champagne blush. She knew that she had to make decisions right away, and her way of doing that usually was to do nothing so that a decision would eventually be forced on her. But this time she knew that wouldn't work. There were only a few options, and she would have to pick one.

All morning she let them spin together, like hers and Hope's clothes rotating in the washer windows of Launder Land. Hope sat on a chair in her new sunsuit and green visor, kicking her feet in time to the washer's rocking rhythm and licking an ice cream in counterpoint. At each change of the cycle, Cassiopeia felt something in herself draining out with the sudsy, gray water. She cleared her throat again and again to remove the lump that kept rising there. And when they had folded and packed their clean clothes into the shopping cart they'd drag back to their room, Cassiopeia looked down at Hope, her face a chocolate blur, and nearly burst into tears.

When they arrived back at their room, it was already noon and the phone was ringing. "Make us some sandwiches, Hopie," she said as she lifted the receiver from its cradle. "Hello."

"Is this Cassiopeia Quinlan?"

"Yes, it is."

"This is Zona's sister, Gail. Marie at the Satellite Lounge gave me your number. She said this was your day off. I hope I'm not bothering you."

"Oh no, not at all. How is Zona?"

"Well, a little better, but it'll take a while for the medication to kick in. I saw her today, and she just wouldn't stop taking about Hope. Look, would it be possible for us to talk in person? I'd love to take you to dinner."

They met at the Velvet Turtle, a restaurant Cassiopeia couldn't usually afford. It was a shadowed, cozy green inside, the carpet thick and lush like a golf course.

"I like this green place," Hope said.

Gail was a slightly older, more elegant version of Zona, with silver-gray, smartly styled hair. She was wearing an expensively quiet slacks set and tinted, designer glasses. "Order whatever you like," she said, "this is my treat."

Cassiopeia ordered prawns and Hope a Turtle-burger. "Zona sure thinks a lot of you both," she began. "You're probably the only friends she has. One of her problems is that she keeps to herself and doesn't tell anybody when she starts needing help."

"Well really, we only just met recently," said Cassiopeia. "Zona helped me get the job at the Satellite. If there's anything I can do to help her now, I'd be happy to."

"Well, as a matter of fact, there just might be. I don't know how long she'll be in the hospital. I guess Marie told you the nature of her illness. They're trying right now just to get her stabilized back on her medica-tion, but the doctor told me today that he wants to keep her a little longer this time. He wants to work on her denial. He thinks she has never really accepted her diagnosis, just goes along with us, and then once she's back to her old self goes off the medication again. I set her up in her little place, and I'd like to keep it so she can go back there when she's discharged. It would be a great help to me if you could just stay there and keep the place up. I'll pay the rent. The doctor thinks it would be a good incentive to Zona if she knew her place was waiting for her."

Cassiopeia was stunned. "Well, to be honest, it would be a great help to me, too. The motel is getting pretty expensive, and so far I haven't saved enough to move."

"Leave everything to me," Gail said. Then, as she was slipping her Visa card under the check, she looked over at Hope. "She's a cute child," she said cooly, smoothing her linen slacks and standing up. Cassiopeia accepted a lift back to the motel, since the light was already draining away. A pearly salmon streaked the horizon and lit the undersides of low scudding clouds.

When Cassiopeia was sure Hope was asleep, she removed three bills from her wallet, dug her address book from out of her purse, and went down to Perkos next door to get change. She ordered a cup of coffee and sat in the gold, tufted booth staring at the cheap floral of her address book. She could have called Hap today, but she didn't. She could have written or called before to give him her address, but she hadn't. It wasn't as if she had made a decision about him, but now, by not acting, one had been made for her.

She opened the book to the S's: Saunders, Skeen, there . . . Skylar. She copied down the number on her coffee-spattered napkin. Her eyes went back up to Saunders. She hadn't thought of Eileen in a while.

Eileen had finally found a good man, Wally Saunders, and then she'd had only close to four good years with him in that trailer park in Bakersfield before cancer took her. At least it happened quickly. Eileen would not have handled suffering well. It was so unexpected, the tears that snuck out so boldly under the hard, jaundiced lights. But they were a salty mixture of all her losses: Eileen, maybe some of Hap, and now Hope. And there was the other loss, the one that had never really been acknowledged but that added its weight to the ledger just the same.

She thought of her father, as she always did, as a mixture of Santa Claus, Paul Bunyan, and God inhabiting some shadowy workshop in another realm where there wasn't anything he couldn't fix. If only Eileen could have told her more about him, but the truth was that she was so embarrassed by how little she remembered or ever knew of him, that she had refused to give more than the barest vignette: he was tall, had brown hair, blue eyes, liked baseball, cars, was a mechanic in the army stationed in France and died in a plane crash during transport. Cassiopeia had always gotten the unspoken message that even these out-of-focus remembrances were a great nuisance and brought back too much pain. Cassiopeia had never had the nerve to ask too many questions, because Eileen seemed to become depressed if the subject were mentioned. Also, Cassiopeia was afraid she might not like the answers. She did not want to believe that maybe her mother hadn't been married at all, and so the complicity gradually became mutual. Cassiopeia left her mind's image of her father in dust and shadows to fade to the merest ghost image, like a badly-developed proof.

Cassiopeia left a dollar bill on the table with her coffee and stayed in the ladies room a good twenty minutes before she could pull herself together enough to make the phone call. The next morning, the bus left her and Hope an hour early at the airport. They sat in the linked row of chairs, watching planes land and feeding quarters into the mini-t.v. Hope pushed buttons, skipping through the channels, delighted at how fast she could make Big Bird switch into the jumping lady in a leotard, who, in turn, jumped into a galloping horse. "That's all the quarters," Cassiopeia said, lifting Hope to her lap. She was small for her four years but still filled up Cassiopeia's lap. "Now, honey, you mind Juanita, you hear. You're just going to visit her for a little while, and when you come back here, we'll get our very own place. Won't that be great? You'll get a room all your own."

Hope looked up at her, mulling this over. "Why can't we get our place now Mommy?"

"Because, honey, I have to save up some money. But now that I'm staying at Zona's, I can save even more."

"Where is Zona?"

"I already told you. She's at the hospital. She's sick, but they're giving her medicine, and she'll get well real soon."

Hope was looking up, studying her mother's face carefully in her child's third eye, reading it for physical signs that might betray the words. She had already learned that words don't always match up with what is happening. Cassiopeia felt small spasms in the muscles of her face. She blinked her eyes hard and smiled at Hope and then hugged her, probably a little too tightly.

"I don't want to go," said Hope, sensing something she didn't really comprehend.

Cassiopeia felt her stomach caving in. The tears were waiting in a place so deep she could probably flood the airport and half the town. She stood up and took Hope's hand.

"Let's get you some snacks for the plane ride. Oh, Hopie, it won't be for long, I promise, and you'll have so much fun. Think of it: Hope Quinlan, globe-trotter, jet-setter. I'll call you every day, and you can write me letters. That'll be fun. Juanita will help you write them."

It wasn't until she watched the plane ripple up into heat waves and become a mere speck in the layers of muddy-looking smog that she let go. She jammed on her sunglasses and made her way, with flooded vision, to the bus stop.

"Two jobs," she thought. "I'll work two jobs, and without paying rent . . ." But she felt scared, more scared than she thought Hope could possibly be. She looked around her. Wives and husbands, grandparents, lovers. It seemed that no one was as alone as she. On the bus she opened a magazine to "Monaco's Royal Family: Who Will Inherit the Throne?"

Cassiopeia spent the rest of the afternoon settling into Zona's small rented house. Zona had stripped off all the window curtains, blankets, sheets, and linens throughout the house and piled them by the washer. She had apparently been in the throes of a manic cleaning marathon, but much of it was still half-done. Cassiopeia washed and hung out the linens, and finished what she could. By night, she fell into bed, almost too exhausted to sleep. She dreamed that she was at a baseball game on a darkened field. She made a base hit and got on second base, but it was dark and scary out there. Then she was in the stands, sucking her thumb, and she suddenly realized that all these people could see her. She tried to climb down the bleachers but couldn't get through the people. Bud Hesparian was there in the stands and suddenly had his hand over the top of her head, pushing her down. She was trying to pry his fingers off but couldn't and fainted. When she came to, she was holding a chubby baby with red hair and freckles and playing with him and laughing. He began to get smaller and smaller and was turning blue until he was almost like a fetus. She took him to a doctor who began working, trying to resuscitate him, and it seemed the baby would come back to life, but the doctor was very angry and yelling at her. She looked down to see that she was wearing a nurse's uniform, and it was all torn and bloodied. She wanted to change her clothes and got on an elevator to go get a fresh uniform but each time the elevator stopped, it was caught between the floors .

Chapter 8
•
Chevyville, Illinois

It was the summer Cassiopeia turned eight. Archie, the town's mental case had raped a teacher, Miss Spoin, in her own garage one night when she returned home from a Tupperware party. They sent Archie away somewhere, and no one ever saw him again. Cassiopeia wrote every day in a five-year diary with a tiny lock and key.

Dear Diary
    Today we ate watermelon and sold our pop bottles, and I got 20¢ for mine. I watch *December Bride* and *It's Always Jan* and they were very funny.

Dear Diary
    Guess what? I am going to be a gril scout. Mama and Wanita are going to be scout leaders cuz nobody wants to do it. We are going to Moline to get my gril dress tomorrow and the hat and socks

too. I almost got my babysitting badge.

The badges were half-dollar size circles, embroidered with scenes representing the different areas: cooking, camping, science, first aid. There was a list of tasks to complete for each badge. At least twenty hours had to be documented and signed by an adult to earn the babysitting badge. It had a little brick house with a baby carriage in front and even though Cassiopeia hated babysitting, she lusted after that badge. She almost didn't get it though. While she was baby-sitting Jimmy Odle, he snuck outside and stuck the neighbor's garden hose in the window of their new Plymouth Fury and turned the water on. Mrs. Odle found it when she came home. Jimmy had carefully rolled the windows back up, with the hose inside, and the Potter's maroon, velvet upholstery was completely ruined. No one could ever decide who was at fault, Eileen being adamant about it being Mrs. Odle's hose and her kid and therefore her fault. Corky Potter finally settled the whole thing when he got drunk and drove the Fury into a creek a month later, not too long after he got his license.

Dear Diary
Our troop is going camping. Sharon Pickerall was picked for president of gril scouts. It was in the papper .We voted on a name for our troop. It is Troop Moonshine. Phyllis Hankey got killed.

Years later, Cassiopeia would find her diary in a box of old letters and things at Juanita's and wonder who in the world Phyllis Hankey was and how she was killed.

It was Juanita's idea for the camping trip. She delved into scout lore, excited about camping tricks. They collected tall juice cans to use as small stoves. The idea was to cut holes out of the bottom for draw, build a tiny fire under the can, and cook the pancakes or eggs on top. They practiced trail marking and identifying animal footprints. They learned camp songs and divided into pairs, splinting each other's arms with rulers and pantomiming what to do for snake bite.

Juanita worked a deal with the American Legion to borrow the retired ambulance they used to deliver chairs for meetings and lectures. They loaded all their camping gear, tents, sleeping bags, and air matresses into the ambulance, and the girls climbed in. Juanita drove. She never knew how it happened, but while passing another car, she hit a button, and the siren came on, causing all the other cars to pull over for them.

"Do something!" yelled Eileen.

The girls squealed happily. Juanita cussed and pounded on every knob, but on they flew, siren blasting a clear path all the way to Camp Towatopotome, or Camp Two On the Potty, as Juanita called it.

In all their weeks of preparation, no one had thought to practice putting up tents, so when they got all the poles, flaps, and canvas laid out, no one knew what to do. Juanita and Eileen floundered for most of the afternoon until some Eagle Scouts from a nearby camp offered to help. Juanita did not turn down their help but later maintained they would have gotten it anyway. After the tents were up, Juanita crawled inside one of them and fell asleep.

The girls were starting to bicker and pick fights, so Eileen took them hiking to look for animal tracks and Indian beads. When they got back to camp, it was discovered that Jeannie Witt was splotched with poison ivy all over her torso. Juanita had managed to kindle a small fire, but it kept going out. So they made bologna sandwiches for supper. They tried singing around the cold campfire, but this didn't last long. There was so much shivering and complaining that finally Juanita just marched them off to their tents. Not finding any gauze, she taped Kotex napkins around Jeannie Witt's hands so she couldn't scratch the runny lumps in her sleep. Used to hot baths and warm beds, the girls couldn't fall asleep, and as a last resort Juanita put them all in the ambulance with their sleeping bags.

"Damn, I hope we can get some peace now," she said to Eileen after shutting the ambulance doors. It was roughly an hour or so later, when Juanita had just drifted off, that Eileen woke her.

"Someone's screaming. Sounds like it's coming from the ambulance." They grabbed flashlights and hurried into the thick tickling of the woods, filled now with the cries of seven hysterical Girl Scouts. Juanita threw open the door of the ambulance.

"What is going on here?"

Jeannie Witt, the only one not crying or screaming, wiped her nose with a Kotex paw. "We were telling ghost stories and Mary Louise saw feet," she simpered.

Juanita located Mary Louise Hickox with her flashlight. She was scrunched against the padded door, her feet sticking out of her sleeping bag, half-moaning, half-sobbing as she pointed to them.

"I see feet. I see feet."

"For crying out loud," said Juanita disgustedly, "they're your own damn feet!"

When the first liquid threads of light trickled through the trees, the girls were up, noses running into white balloons of their breath, demanding to eat. Juanita spoke to no one but swirled eggs fiercely in a bowl while Eileen set up the juice can stoves. But when the pancake batter and eggs did nothing but sit pitifully on the tops of the cans, the little fires underneath sputtering and puffing out, no one would even look at Juanita. With nothing else to eat but a few bags of marshmallows, they loaded the ambulance and headed for home, Jeannie Witt scratching rythmically in the sniffling gloom.

Finally Juanita said, "Why is everyone so quiet? You'd think we were going to a funeral or something. Who wants to stop for doughnuts?"

Cassiopeia sat in the back of the ambulance next to Jeannie Witt because no one else had wanted to sit beside her, and Eileen had finally put Cassiopeia there to end the fussing over who was to sit where. Cassiopeia had felt the strain from the first of having her mother and aunt as leaders. It was the preacher's kid syndrome: a secret resentment whether the kid behaved or not or got special favors or not and a no-win situation for the kid.

Cassiopeia thought she would befriend Jeannie

Witt, who was an outcast at the moment because of her condition, but when she offered Jeannie a dough-nut hole, she shook her head and said loftily, "I saw your Aunt Juanita smoking."

Cassiopeia said nothing, but all the way home she hated Eileen. It proved to be the last ride of troop Moonshine, however. The mothers were pretty upset. Two girls had bad head colds, Jeannie Witt's eyes swelled shut, and Mary Louise Hickox had to sleep with a light on for weeks after.

Chapter 9
·
Fresno, California

It was always time to go to work it seemed to Cassiopeia, and, in fact, it was. She still pulled the eleven to six shift at the Satellite and now worked for a janitorial service from seven till one. She had tried working the late shift for awhile and taking a day job at Lynette's Fashions, but after three weeks she was tired, run-down, and snappy with the Satellite's customers. Marie had taken her aside and given her the number of the janitorial service.

"Working with the public's hell, girl," she said, "and you're asking for double trouble. If you gotta work two jobs, give yourself a break. I don't need another girl goin' off cuckoo on me."

Marie was pretty much running the Satellite now that Bud was bogged down in court hearings and in his new playmate, Yolanda, who demanded a change of scene every week-end and dinners out in between. No one at the Satellite missed Bud, either.

Marie had said, "Bud wouldn't do Jesus Christ a favor for eternal salvation in return."

Cassiopeia took a quick shower between jobs so

she could just fall into bed when she got home from work after midnight. She was drying off in the darkened bedroom and caught sight of herself in the mirror. "Well, I don't have to worry about running to fat these days," she thought. Her ribs stuck out like an unplayed harp. Her joints were like door knobs beneath the stretched skin. She came from a long line of scrawny, Southern women. But she didn't have further time to reflect and pulled on her jeans and t-shirt, stuck her long hair in a pony tail, and grabbed a bagel, her dinner, on her way out.

She had found an old filing cabinet-gray Toyota and bought it for two hundred dollars. The door on the passenger side didn't open, and it had no reverse, but otherwise was in great condition and never failed to start. She just had to be careful where she parked it, always sliding into the space nearest the corner when she parked along the curb or pointing the hood outward in parking lots. But she needed a car now that she worked two jobs.

When she got to work, she unlocked the office door and slipped inside, going first to the radio and turning it up to Aretha Franklin's "Respect," doing a few turns around the floor with the dust mop. She then unlocked the cabinet with another key from her hoop of keys and pulled out a vacuum cleaner and cleaning supplies. She made a note of the time, wanting to break her old record tonight. She got paid for six hours work but could go whenever she was done. Her last record was four hours, fifty-two minutes.

She had a complex of offices to do, and she had to vacuum, dust, dump ashtrays, and clean bathrooms.

When she finished, she locked everything up and stepped into the night's mimosa breezes. These blistering summer days were redeemed only by the night's cool atonement. Cassiopeia liked driving home at this hour, mentally tabulating her savings to the blink, blink of her turn signal. The darkened neighborhoods closed into themselves, and the the stores were brightly lit and empty.

She would not allow herself to think of Hope until she was home, where her bedtime ritual included adding lines to the serial letter she mailed off to Hope twice a week. But tonight there was a new billboard at the stoplight where she turned off to head south for home. It was a frail smudge of a girl about Hope's age with large, frighteningly luminous eyes asking who cared enough to send money for her next meal. Cassiopeia made the turn in a blur of tears. Lately it was as if her emotions ruled in a garden irrigated by a vast seedbed of tears. Just the other day it had been a commercial for homeless pets that set her off.

The next morning, she woke already sticky at eight-thirty, knowing it would be hot. Cassiopeia turned on the radio and t.v. "I want noise," she thought. "Noise enough to drown my thoughts."

At the Satellite Lounge, it was falsely still before the five o'clock happy hour storm, but Cassiopeia had two stiffs by four-thirty. "Is there some new law against tipping in hot weather?" she asked Marie.

"There oughta just be a law against this weather," answered Marie.

The Satellite was not a big place and when it was busy, a crowd collected fast. Cassiopeia wove through the happy hour bodies, plunking foamy mugs of beer and cocktails down on napkins, snapping out change and bills. Marie said she was the fastest changer in the West with her inherited calculating abilities.

"Even my mother-in-law drinks a cold beer in this weather," Bill was saying.

"Hey, did you hear about that serial killer in L.A.? Goes after lingerie sales ladies. Disguises himself as a woman, goes in to try on a girdle, waits till she comes in by herself, and then, BOINGO!" Ray Miller loved these grisly stories.

"Hey, that guy gives serial killers a bad name," said Bill.

Cassiopeia didn't want to hear any more and scooted off after counting out their change. It was hours later while she was waiting for the three secretaries to decide on a drink that she looked up and saw him. At first she wasn't sure. He looked like any other happy hour cowboy, roping beers, hooking his boots on a chair rung. There was no sign that he had seen her. He was with an older man dressed entirely in leather, and leaning back under the gravity of a well-inflated spare tire with the look of one resisting a sales pitch. Ned Quinlan looked much the same, his reddish, blonde hair maybe a little longer. At some point, Cassiopeia had given up her search for Ned, not consciously, but she'd stopped looking and, therefore, had stopped thinking about him or Hap. The motive that had driven her to Fresno just disappeared.

Cassiopeia took off for the kitchen, almost colliding head on with Marie. "Hey, the speed limit's fifty-five here. You're doin' about eighty," Marie said.

"I just saw him," Cassiopeia said.

"Who's him? The night stalker?"

"Worse. It's Ned. He's out there. My husband. What'll I do?"

"Well, you'll ask him if he wants another drink. He is a customer, Cassie. Look, just be real cool, and don't let him suck you into anything."

"Oh shit!" Cassiopeia said as she let out her breath and pushed through the swinging doors. Ned seemed to be intently trying to convince the leather-dudded man about something and didn't see Cassiopeia as she came up to their table.

"Can I get you fellas anything else?" It must have been her voice, because Ned's cowboy hat popped up. "Cass-E-O-peia," he said.

"He still can't say my name right," she thought.

Ned was stretching in his old, sleepy way, smiling his lazy mutt smile. Cassiopeia wondered if drugs made people unaware of the passage of time. Ned behaved as if she had left him an hour ago to use the ladies room and just now returned. What she had planned to say deserted her like a whistle in the dark. The leather man coughed hurriedly.

"Oh yes. Cassie, this is Cal Sunderland, my future manager."

Cal tipped his leather hat and drawled, "Pleasure, Miss. That's still to be settled, Wade."

Ned looked a bit sheepish. "My new stage name. Wade Tildawn," he explained. "I'm playing a Thursday and Friday night gig over at the T-Bone Tavern with the boys. Call ourselves the Midnight Cowboys . . . whole new band, Cassie. Hey, why don't you come on over and catch us this week?"

"Nice to meet you, Mr. Sunderland," she said. Then to Ned, "I have to work. Speaking of work, as you can see," she said, waving through the noise and smoke, "we're real busy."

"Nothing more for me," said Cal Sunderland, folding a ten dollar bill into her hand. "Keep the change, Miss. Look, Wade, I'll be callin' you before end a' the week."

Ned leaped up, started to say something, then slithered back. "O.K. Mr. Sunderland. You can leave a message, if I'm not in, or you can always call me at the T-Bone."

This last line was thrown at Cal Sunderland as his neon-striped, leather back was heading out the door.

"I have to get back to work Ned," Cassiopeia said. "I would like to talk to you though. Business," she added firmly.

"What time do you get off?"

"I have another job after this," she said, though this was her day off and she'd just come in to work extra hours at the Satellite. "How about tomorrow morning, eleven o'clock, at Perko's on Blackstone?" She wanted some time to think about what she needed to say.

Ned took a slow draw on the cigarette he'd just lit. "I got to rehearse tomorrow. Can't you tell me what this is about?"

"Look, I didn't want to blurt this out here, but I want to start divorce proceedings. Can you blame me? Never mind. Just write your number down and I'll have a lawyer contact you . . . "

"Hey, Cassie, don't get sore. O.K.? Look, I'll get rehearsal changed. O.K. Perko's tomorrow, ten o'clock."

"Eleven!" Cassiopeia nearly screeched, looking up then to see Bud, recently arrived in his usual white flashiness and black mood, glaring from behind the bar at her. Bud could move very fast for an old ferrett and was beside her in a puff of cigar smoke, sprinkling starry ashes on her feet. "You've been at this table now for fifteen mintues, Mrs. Quinlan. Get your ass movin', or I'm gonna light a fire under it for you." He waggled his cigar at the back side of her skirt.

Why this set Ned off she would never know. Maybe it was just an excuse for a fight that had long been brewing inside him. Maybe he'd just lived his life too long in too many loser, cruiser bars. But like a reflex action, Ned defiantly pointed the red, drooping ash of his cigarette and flicked it smack onto Bud's crisply tailored shirt. Despite his Lilliputian-dude look, Bud had the heart of a scrapper and had been his own bouncer years before he had smartened up the old, bad dog bar image to its present Satellite Lounge fake elegance.

"Look at the shrimp in a pimp suit," Ned spit into the sudden quiet.

"Why you damn redneck! Get outta my . . . "

Bud didn't finish. He threw his full bantum whiteness at Ned, who had swiveled by now out of the booth and landed backside on the dime-sized dance floor with Bud clinging to his neck. Ned swung clumsily at Bud and missed. Bud's fist jabbed out, a pale mosquito, drawing from somewhere on Ned's face blood that tossed up a bright red confetti onto Bud's white shirt.

Ned was swinging wild and frantic now, Bud backing him the whole while out the door. Ned managed to hook into Bud's face on the right side, crunching his cheekbone and cracking his glasses apart just as they crossed the threshold into the parking lot. Bud grunted even more fiercely and cannon-balled his whole body at Ned. Ned must have gotten to his car after that, because all they could hear were the sounds of a revved engine and shouts and insults volleyed back and forth.

Cassiopeia had taken refuge with Marie behind the bar. Marie had set her on a stool, one hand protectively on her shoulder, the other clapped over her own mouth, until she'd heard the unmistakable cracking of bone. Then she went to dial 9-1-1 for an ambulance. Cassiopeia remained on the stool, saying nothing, dissolving into anger. She had heard Ned scream something from outside: "... teach you ... my wife ..."

"Well, that's it for me," she said deflatedly to Marie.

"You don't think Bud knew Ned was your husband before?"

"Well, whatever, he sure knows now."

"Why don't you go home, Cassie. Skip out the back door, kid. I've called an ambulance for Bud. I think I hear it now. I better go out there. I'll do what I can for you." Marie was at the door, attempting to block the path of craning customers.

Cassiopeia snuck out the back, got into her car and switched on the ignition, but could go nowhere without backing up and away from the crowd that Marie had unsuccessfully herded away from the scene. Paramedics now huddled around Bud Hesparian, his immaculate whites dappled with blood, neon, and a bath of red light from the ambulance. Cassiopeia rolled down her window a sliver and could hear Marie's competent voice soothing Bud, patiently urging him into the ambulance. As it pulled out of the parking lot and tore into the night, the spectators began to drift back to their melting drinks, clearing a path for Cassiopeia to head dispiritedly home.

Sitting at Perko's the next morning, Cassiopeia saw no headlines in the morning edition of the newspaper of last night's skirmish. There was just a note under SIRENS: "9:22 p.m. Cocktail lounge owner at 630 N. Palm suffered dislocated jaw and required stitches after fight attempting to remove patron." She ordered coffee and an English muffin and wondered why she was there. It was highly unlikely that Ned would show up. However, at about ten after eleven, just when she was preparing to leave, she saw his black cowboy hat bobbing at the door. His face was a map of bruises and swellings. One eye was swollen partially shut.

"Well, I didn't think you'd show up," she said.

Ned signaled for coffee and grunted as he folded himself stiffly into the booth. "Son of a bitch, Cassie, I'm s'posed to play tomorrow night. Look at me. How can I . . ."

Cassiopeia interrupted him. "I probably don't have a job at all now. What about that? Not only do you not support your daughter or even help, now you've caused me to lose my job so I can't support her. Is that your goal in life? To see your daughter starving and penniless?" She stopped. She hadn't intended to go off like that, but his self-centeredness made her crazy. "And what about Hope? You haven't even asked about her at all. Don't you . . ."

"I guess I figured I didn't even have the right to ask about her . . . thought you'd tell me she was none of my business, and you'd be right."

Cassiopeia sighed. "Jeeze, Ned. I'm not a monster."

"Well, I ain't either," he said. "I'm a no good son-of-a-bitch, but I'm not a monster. So, how is Hope?"

"She's fine, I guess. She's with her godmother in Illinois. I've been working two jobs trying to bring her back and get our own place."

"Guess I screwed everything up for you as usual."

"Guess you did." Then she softened some. "Oh, look, Ned. Forget it. Maybe it's just time for me to leave the Satellite anyway. Bud's a real pig. You couldn't have picked a better creep to beat up on. But it looks like you got the worst of it."

"You may not believe this, Cassie, but I'm sorry about your job and well, for everything. All I've ever wanted to do was play my guitar and sing cowboy songs." This was really the first time they had ever talked like this, with this much honesty.

"Ned, I've wondered about something for a long time." She paused, surprised at her own courage. "Ned, why did you marry me anyway?"

He stirred two creams and three sugars into his coffee, swirled it a long while then looked up. "I'm always doing things that I wake up to next day not knowing how they came about. I'm used to it now, and I've learned to walk away and not turn back. It's just how I am." He paused, looking at her long, and slow. "The real question is why did you marry me?"

"When I was in school they always said, 'You can do anything you want. Just do your best and never give up. Work hard and you can make your dreams come true.' Well, I believed all that, and I thought everytime that if I'd just try harder I could make it work. Nothing in my life had ever turned out that way, but I still wanted to believe. The worse you were, the more determined I'd become. " Cassiopeia shook her head slowly. "I guess all I ever wanted was to find the right cowboy. Well, now I'm not so sure. I think I've spent my life chasing down shadows that couldn't be caught, living someone else's life, like a character in a book. All I know right now, is I want to get a divorce, to get on with my own life."

"Whatever you want, Cassie, Where do I sign?"

"Two things, Ned. I want two things from you. I have to see the lawyer yet, but you can't disappear on me again. I've got to be able to find you when the papers are ready. The other thing is I want full custody of Hope and for you to sign papers relinquishing any claim to her in any way and stating that you won't interfere in her life or try to see her."

Ned scratched the whiskers on his chin. "Sounds O.K. for now. But what if I feel different later?"

"That's precisely what I want to avoid. I want to start a new life for Hope and I don't want ANYBODY interfering. You haven't paid any . . ."

Ned interrupted her. "O.K. Cassie. I know I haven't done much for either of you. If that's what you want, that's the least I could do. I'd just like to think some day I could do something for her."

"You can right now. You can give her a life with some stability, some history, and that'll happen best if you stay out of the picture." There wasn't much more for him to say. "Ned," she said, "I don't believe all that crap anymore about hard work and doing your best."

"So, what are you gonna do? Rob a bank?"

"Course not. But I just don't want money ruling my life, and it is now, because I don't have it. I do wish you the best of luck. I hope you make it, Ned."

Ned's eyes had begun to hover over the booth just beyond them where three girls were oozing make-up, giggles, and young adult hormones. Cassiopeia left him blowing streams of smoke in their direction, telling the waitress he'd gotten those "nasty bruises" falling off his horse, and wouldn't she like to hear him play at the T-Bone sometime.

After she was outside, she opened the flyer he'd given her. In rope-like lettering above a photograph were the words WADE TILDAWN AND THE MIDNIGHT COWBOYS. And there he was with long hair, soft sprouts of sideburns, chin whiskers, and a satin, fringed cowboy shirt, surrounded by his band with a backdrop of Xeroxed stars. At the bottom, he had scribbled two telephone numbers where she could be sure to reach him or to at least leave a message.

When Cassiopeia got home, she pulled on an old, baggy sundress and lay down in the bedroom, still closed up to the light. She felt so incredibly tired in a delicious sort of way. She was beginning to like sleep in a way she never had before. Since adulthood, sleep had become an annoyance, like a pesky, nipping dog, always in the way when she was busy and nowhere to be seen if she wanted company. Now it just came ambling on all fours, old and comfortable, staying out of her way until she called, and it nuzzled up to her softly then in darkness.

When she awoke she lay quietly, feeling as if she were stuck to the bed. Someone was hammering nearby, a sound that always put her back in the shade of the roof where Red's shadow marked the top of the world, where the echoes of pounding echoed themselves, and where the sun was a precious stone set in the massive buckle of his cowhide belt. Why Red should come into her thoughts like this, she didn't know. Over the years he had wandered in and out, a gigantic, hovering red ghost, his pointed cowboy boot toes just above her tilted-back head. Perhaps, she thought, he was the most tangible representation of a father she'd known, even though she never attached that word to him. Even Wally, later, could not assume that position.

"Curious," she thought, "how I never realized the similarities between Red and Ned before."

Perhaps they'd both given her something, a piece of the puzzle that was herself, though it was still incomplete, like the ones they had dragged with them from town to town, thousand-piece jigsaws. With every move, a different piece was lost . . . sunk deep into the lint womb between the cushions of a stuffed sofa; skittered down the grates of a floor furnace to nest with the mice; under the kitchen sink, faded and warped, between the Comet and the Future floor wax.

She thought of a needlepoint tapestry Eileen had begun when she was very small, a blurry forest of pine trees, a mottled brook, and two spotted deer, one bent to water, the other staring straight ahead in fear and recognition. It was never finished but was folded into tissue paper and a Christmas box for each move. Cassiopeia had found it when she went through Eileen's things for Wally. It was still in its box, buried beneath an avalanche of unused fabric and creased wrapping paper stored in Eileen and Wally's mobile home. This more than anything had given her pain, had caused an ache that seemed almost physical. She'd set it aside to take home and later burned it in a metal basin on the postage stamp-sized patio of her apartment. There was nothing else to do with it, since she could neither bear to look at it nor to have anyone finish it. Cassiopeia thought now of all the loose ends, parts that didn't fit, the diary pages unfinished, the doors not closed, the passageways she kept falling down, passageways to nowhere. Seeing Ned that morning had helped in some way she couldn't define, helped her to see where she had to go next and how to get there. The phone was ringing. It felt as if it, too, had been sweating when she picked it up.

"Hi, Cassie." It was Marie. "I just talked to Bud. He's pissed off plenty, but I think if you lay low for about a week, he'll get over it. He really doesn't want to be bothered with hiring someone new right now. My cousin said she'd come in for a week, but she doesn't want the job. She's looking for a cosmetology position. Just got her license. So, we'll just start you back in a week. He'll be cooled off by then, and the swelling will have gone down." Then she added, "His head was already swollen enough if you ask me."

Cassiopeia was feeling relieved enough to joke about it all. "Bad luck is like the I.R.S.," Red had once said. "Once it gets your number, it'll dog you for all your worth."

That same day she talked to Marie, the janitorial service manager called telling her she was being tempor-arily laid off, and he didn't know for sure how long . . . "maybe a month, maybe just a couple of weeks." He said they had lost some accounts, schedules were being rearranged, and she was low person on the totem pole. He said he was sorry, but it was out of his control.

When Cassiopeia said she had to have a pay-check, what did they expect her to do, he just said, "do whatever you have to do." When she hung up the phone, she felt a weariness that went beyond the physical. There was no one to blame, no one to cry to. She felt the collective defeat of generations of those caught at the bottom of the heap. She felt trapped there, the fight seeping out of her amid the deadening claustro-phobia of fear.

The next few days, she did not leave the house. She ate carelessly, whatever she happened to find in the fridge. She slept, bathed, drank a ton of coffee, and wandered from room to room as if her mind had been put on hold. The phone rang once, and she didn't answer.

The third morning was cooler. Cassiopeia rose early. The light this time of day fell on walls, floors, fences, walkways, like a fresh coat of paint. It was a time to notice things, the sweet gossip of birds whispering tree to tree, the silver unravelling of snails now coiled into their shells asleep after a night of waving their antennae at the moon, the faint breath of new blooming phlox.

Cassiopeia took her cup of coffee into the yard and sat in an old straw chair under the apricot tree. Maybe she would pick some apricots and stew them today. Eileen had always loved stewed apricots on toast, she said to herself, all the while knowing she wouldn't do it. She shifted in her chair, the stillness seeping into her very bones. These quiet times were the hardest. She had avoided them almost entirely with work so far. First, she could feel the lump forming in her stomach, and a sourness like old milk, then the tears, not far behind. They came now, hot and fast. She stirred them into her coffee, they ran down her neck. One huge droplet even wet her big toe.

She had planned to have Hope back with her by now, but she hadn't planned on the unforeseen, this enforced vacation, and the other expenses. She'd had to have the car smogged last week, and it had taken five separate tries and a slew of costly repairs she didn't understand to push it through. She had stood there in the grease-carpeted, oil-saturated garage while Joey, a young Mexican boy whose accent even seemed oiled spoke to her in the language of automotives. She wished she knew just one man who would step into this foreign country and deal with mechanics in their own tongue.

She thought of her father, a mechanic. If he

watched somewhere from the dark side of the moon, as she believed as a child, why didn't he send her help in some way. Instead, she just wrote out check after check, subtracting in her head from the projected figure she needed to bring Hope back and set them up. And now, with these new set-backs . . .

Cassiopeia wiped her eyes on her kimono sleeve, fumbled in the pocket for a Kleenex, and blew her nose. She had given in to the urge to call Hope on a weekday several times, and after she got the phone bill had vowed not to do that anymore. Every daily expense was accounted for in the master plan she carried in her head and transformed into calculations, plus or minus.

The vapor trail of a jet streaked up overhead, engines blowing over the small sounds around her. Little by little, Cassiopeia had come to an awareness of what Hope's not being there meant. From the moment Hope had been placed in her arms, Cassiopeia had been aware mostly of the responsibility, of how the full weight of that small, hungry, helpless being was in her hands alone. Love and fear had always been coexistent for her, with either one bringing the expectation of the other, so that even the new, incomparable waves of love that crashed over her when she held Hope were also fear-inducing.

All of her resources seemed to go into caretaking. There was never much time to sit and play with Hope, to just enjoy watching her. Cassiopeia was always picking her up or dropping her off, working, shopping, or mixing formula, always in a hurry. Slowly now, Cassiopeia was becoming aware of a whole new means of existence, like that child she'd read about in the newspaper who'd finally been rescued from the box he had been kept in for six years. She could imagine how — raised always in a narrow, confining and false environment— frightening and amazing the world he escaped into must appear to him. There would be so much that experience had never provided as fuel for his imagination.

She thought of how her life had, in smaller measure, been that way. There was so much lacking, and not knowing had kept even her dreams narrowed. Her childhood had been absent of zoos, music, dancing lessons, pets, brothers or sisters and family vacations. But there had been libraries, and somewhere between alchemy and zygosis, she had read about families and people who live in Paris, go to museums, and name the galaxies. They mixed in her fantasies with Zorro and Mary Queen of Scots, her beautiful twin sister, and her handsome, mechanic father, who invented marvelous machines and could fix anything.

Chapter 10
Chevyville, Illinois

Eileen and Cassiopeia had just returned in the fall to Chevyville after having spent the fith grade school year and summer in Mississippi, where Cassiopeia was a "Yankee" and "the new girl" all year long. But Eileen's returning had more to do with Grady's gall bladder than with Cassiopeia's adjustment, or lack thereof. What with Eileen's lack of observance and Cassiopeia's reticence, her problems remained hidden.

It was the middle of the sixth grade school year, and Cassiopeia walked home with one bobby sock creeping down her leg like a stretched-out caterpillar despite the rubber bands she had anchored it with. The sock puddled around her ankle, and she increased her pace, hoping no one would notice. Paula Palmer had turned her smug nose on Cassiopeia at recess the day before. Paula had radar for anything out of the norm and was self-appointed chief of the social police.

"Why are your teeth funny like that?" she asked Cassiopeia, loud enough to stop the whole playground.

Paula had a long, blonde ponytail, and marbley, blue-rimmed glasses. Cassiopeia wanted to look just like her and had been pulling on her hair to make it grow and reading in dark corners, hoping to ruin her eyes so she could get glasses like Paula's. Paula wore cuffed bobby socks and white bucks. Cassiopeia had asked Eileen for white bucks and new socks. Eileen said O.K. to the socks and then forgot to buy them. She said the white bucks were not practical.

Besides wanting to change every single thing about her looks, Cassiopeia had other worries. The teacher had assigned an essay to be titled "My Family." They were to have a contest, with the four winners receiving gold stars and certificates for ice cream sundaes at Potter's Drug Store. Mrs. Humphrey talked about paragraphs and suggested that each family member could be a paragraph, with introduction and conclusion. "

For example," she said, "if you have four in your family, how many paragraphs would you have? That's right Paula, six paragraphs." They were to tell something about the likes and dislikes, age, description, and occupation of family members. They could add a paragraph for a favorite pet and one to describe the house, if they liked. The teacher explained how when you added all the paragraphs together, you had an essay, just like adding all the people together gave you a family. She seemed pleased with herself when she said this.

There were two in Cassiopeia's family and no pets and right then they were living with Juanita, and she didn't want to describe Juanita's rock-and-bone lined windows, knowing instinctively that this was not like anything the other children lived with. She had seen replicas of their houses on "Father Knows Best" and "Leave it to Beaver," the Pledge-dusted bannisters of carpeted stairs, the oval, braided rug where Skippy dreamed before the hearth while June and Ward conferred about The Beaver. There were no swaying palms on fringed, satin pillows embroidered with FLORIDA, no Bootles Gin vases with peacock feathers fanned in the window, and no tangerine calypso dancers swinging their hips through the rabbit ears on the t.v. set.

Cassiopeia brooded over this essay all week, longer even than she had brooded and worried over her polio shot. If she was sick or late with it, she'd just have to make it up. Mrs. Humphrey was short and ancient with battleship hips and soft, flaccid skin that smelled like a baby's. She clicked her false teeth between words and said, "now pupils" with a *pu* that rhymed with *cue*. She was eternally old and tired, and the students easily persuaded her to give them one more week on their essays.

Cassiopeia spun herself dizzy then lay on her back looking up through chestnut trees that reached upwards to the tipsy sky. She watched the carnival roll of thick clouds on a blue saucer sky. She experimented with opening and shutting her eyes fast, watching the trees flicker. It was then that it came to her like sunlight cutting through lapped branches. She ran into the house and got pencil and paper, carried it back under the tree, and began the first paragraph:

This is the story of my family. We
live in a big, big house that has two

porches and a balconny upstairs.
Everybody has there own room. Now I
will tell you about my family. My father's
name is Carl. How old he is I don't know.

He is tall and likes baseball, his
favorite food is spagettee. He takes me
with him to ride horses. He trains horses
and has to go to different towns all the
time for shows. He likes to talk to my
mom in the living room about my little
brother's problems. But they are not
much really. Like a man sold my brother
skates that are too big once. My brother
is seven years old . . .

She went on to describe a brother with an
uncanny resemblance to Beaver Cleaver and a mom,
whose hobbies were baking cookies and waxing floors.
She conjured up twin sisters named Darla and Carla
and a poodle name Pierre, spelled Peaair. He had been
a circus dog before they got him and could walk on two
legs and jump through hoops. Cassiopeia decided to
give Juanita a paragraph, saying that she was her mother's sister, a swimming teacher visiting from Florida.
She imagined Florida as all one beach; therefore, it was
Juanita's only possible occupation.

All together, Cassiopeia had nine paragraphs
and was quite pleased with the essay. She went back
and checked all her spelling in the dictionary. If Mrs.
Humphrey had been more aware, not quite so ancient
and naive, perhaps she would have questioned at least
some of this. But the lies were all plausible, if not prob-

able, and the essay was so well-written that she chose it, along with three others, to tack on the bulletin board, each with a big, fat red A+ and a gold star.

But Fate intervened disfavorably by marking Paula Palmer's essay with an alarming B+, probably her first ever.

Mrs. Humphrey, myopically oblivious to the social order of her students or their grade histories, could never be accused of playing favorites. Paula burst into tears when her paper was passed back and refused to speak all through recess, circled by her gang of girls who, puzzled by her pouting, gingerly questioned her, offering her extra turns and hushed sympathy, completely mystified by her mute grief. Paula knew how to play them, knew instinctively that by keeping her calamity a mystery, it would be less easily dismissed and in the process, could garner increased attention for her.

Paula was the rallying point for every minor or major event of their grammar school world. It was not just the blonde ponytail and brains — though that could be disputed, since what good student isn't always perceived as smarter than everyone else in everything — Paula had IT and she didn't have to lift a finger or whisper a prayer to earn IT. Paula was born with IT and would go through life beloved by teachers, adored and envied by classmates, and always, always, always encouraged and expected to succeed.

Cassiopeia felt only mildly guilty for her A+. After all, wasn't the assignment really a test of their writing abilities? But she was not prepared for the next morning at school. When she arrived, the girls in

Paula's crowd had been reading the winning essays out loud to each other and had discovered immediately what Mrs. Humphrey, in her naive blindness had not discerned. When Cassiopeia came in, they all stopped talking and exchanged looks. One giggled and another shushed her. Cassiopeia could feel the warmth flooding up her neck.

At recess, there was more whispering and a subtle kind of avoidance. And later, a note was jammed under her math book: "Show us your trick dog. LIAR!" Many years later, Cassiopeia would look back and see how the rest of the school year turned on that gold star, and that even though she did get her A+ and ice cream certificate and won the contest and was not found out by Mrs. Humphrey or Eileen, there was another, more terrible and exacting toll to be paid.

Her status of marginal acceptance in Paula's crowd dropped even lower, making her even more shy and withdrawn. This, in turn, encouraged their further alienation, and on and on it went until she had the complete status of non-status. Years later, she would visualize the row of essays plastered to that wall and the gold star — a tribute that remained unseen by Eileen — briefly blazing with a cold, hard light before blurring away in a streak of glory and despair.

Chapter 11
Fresno, California

As she stepped into the night for a quick smoke, Cassiopeia gazed up at the stars, wondering how many of them were already gone, leaving the flare of their last light like the after-image of doused candles. She had read about dead stars still sending their light earthward in a *National Geographic* she'd found on Zona's coffee table. The lush stars made her think how wide the universe was and how little she knew of it.

She had been cooped up for so long that she felt like an alien from outer space. Today she had spoken to the mailman, her first human contact in almost a week, and her simple "Good morning. How are you?" had been almost frighteningly painful. She could hear the neighbor's t.v. babbling. It was a program on Amelia Earhart citing new findings to explain the mystery of her disappearance. All Cassiopeia remembered about Amelia Earhart from school was how it was believed that she had flown her plane into the sun. Later, on the playground, Cassiopeia had pumped hard on the swing, pushing out with her scabbed and skinny legs, flying higher and higher, thinking she too could soar high enough to burst through the sun. Once, she had gone almost as high as the top bar, scared herself and then stopped.

The next morning as she dressed, she decided she had to force herself to go out or she'd go nuts. There was a branch library about twelve blocks away, and she could cut through the park on the way. It didn't take long to reach the graceful estate-like grounds of Roeding Park with its immense trees, rich, green lawns, duck ponds, tennis courts, and a small playland maintained by the Rotary Club.

The day was clear and windless. Cassiopeia breathed in the sweetness of pine and wet grass. When she came to the playland, her first thought was of Hope. Too bad she'd never brought her here. Only a few of the rides were engaged. The merry-go-round and the small Ferris wheel each had a number of smiling passengers, and the toy airplanes were spinning baby circles for two fat toddlers, one teething on the steering wheel. The bright tea cups were frozen, tipped at odd angles, as if left there from a rowdy tea party.

Cassiopeia bought a Coke from a skinny, tattooed man whose smile revealed his bad teeth. She sat on a bench, the merry-go-round plinking out a tinny tune, and watched the Ferris wheel creak and dip in the wind. Now there was only one passenger, a blonde boy about twelve who looked as if he should have been in school. Cassiopeia watched the baskets swing in the wind as the shiny wheel swept upwards toward the treetops.

When she was a child, she loved the carnival that came to Chevyville every year, especially the Ferris wheel. She hoarded, begged, and scavenged money for weeks to blow on the fleeting rides and cheap, shiny prizes. Always, she went by herself. Eileen had no interest in going.

Once she had been at the very apex of the Ferris wheel's rotation when it stopped. There was some mechanical problem. Two teenage girls just below her began screaming. Far below, the carnival men ran back and forth for at least fifteen, maybe twenty, minutes. At first Cassiopeia had been scared, but after awhile, she began to like it. She could see the lights trailing clear across town, the minute people below pointing upwards. Cooler air whipped softly through her hair. She let the basket rock then, nudging it forward and back with her body's weight. She did not feel stuck at all but liberated from that dull sameness that waited for her below. As the gondola swayed, she sang her favorite song:

"Would you like to swing on a star?
Carry moonbeams home in a jar?
And be better off than you are . . .
Yes, you can be better than you are
You can be swinging on a star."

Time became a dark window between the present and the past, and she became part of a river of luminous clouds trapped there, fluid and continuous. When they had finally made the repairs and her car was brought down, the bar unlocked and thrown over her head, and her feet were back on the spongey ground, she had not felt relief at all but an immense disappointment.

"Scuse me, scuse me, . . . Miss. . ." Cassiopeia looked up, torn away from the past, to a man in a magenta leisure suit who was leaning toward her. His pants rode up, revealing the yellowy band of ankle between sock and calf. He had pale olive skin, slightly slanted eyes, a large, pitted nose, and could have been any nationality from Greek to Puerto Rican, Italian, Armenian, or any combination. "Did you work over at da Real Office on Mildreda?"

"No, I didn't." Cassiopeia struck a tone of voice that was not unfriendly but not encouraging.

"Is you da girl that was da RE-ceptionist?"

"No, definitely not."

"You not Alicia den?" He spoke a black dialect, but didn't seem to be black.

"I'm sorry, but no, I'm not." The friendly tone was slipping.

"I beg your pardon den. Must be a case of MIS-taken identity." He bowed quite formally and sauntered away. Cassiopeia stood up herself. She could see it was time to move along.

"What could that poor soul have wanted?" she wondered as she crossed the railroad tracks of the toy train that looped through the park. She headed out of the park and into the blur of traffic. "If that was a pick-up line, it was pretty pitiful. Or did he really think she was Alicia? Maybe," she mused, "I am Alicia and just don't know it. Maybe I had been Alicia at one time. Maybe, when I stepped off that Ferris wheel, I gave up Alicia's life. Maybe we step from one life to another without ever knowing, like traveling through paralell universes. Maybe, somewhere, I walk in Alicia's shoes, dream Alicia's dream, wind Alicia's wristwatch. Maybe this is actually Alicia's dream, and I'm merely part of it." She waited at the corner of Olive and Weber, the cars blazing past, the drivers bent to the speed of their destinies, on their way to work, to buy milk and razor blades, to rob banks, to have secret affairs.

Cassiopeia looked up. The sun was breaking through a ring of clouds on its habitual journey across the sky, one of the many hostages held in this collusion that everyone had agreed to call "time."

Chapter 12

•

Los Angeles, California

Cassiopeia never knew when or why Eileen would decide to pick up and go, and she usually found out about it in some incidental way: "Oh, Cassie, pick up some film while you're at Walgreens. We're takin' off for L.A. next week."

Cassiopeia often protested, if only for the sake of the disruption, but this time, although she was fearful of change, she was unhappy enough at school that L.A. sounded exciting and glamorous. For a short while after they arrived in Los Angeles, they lived with the Schrams, Jehovah's Witnesses Eileen met on the Greyhound. Eileen had picked L.A. because she had a brief notion of breaking into movies, probably encouraged by Juanita. She even took acting lessons at a seedy little acting school that catered to the star-struck. But the lessons didn't last long, because the Witnesses talked her out of it as too evil and wordly an occupation for a lady.

The Schram's daughter, Sharon, was only a few years older than Cassiopeia but twice her size, almost mute, and fully developed. She wore tinkling charm bracelets so loaded with gaudy charms that they looked like they weighed at least three pounds, and her makeup appeared to have been applied with a spatula. Witnesses could wear make-up, Sharon said, but not celebrate birthdays, and she had to read the ingredients label on candy bars to "make sure there's no blood in it." The Witnesses knew that unscrupulous candy manufacturers tried to sneak it in. They could eat meat, though, which Cassiopeia never understood.

To appease the Witnesses, Eileen began Bible study with them in the evenings and attended church with the Schrams on Sundays. Cassiopeia was dragged along in sullen but silent protest. She would find herself often drifting away from the sermon, the dinner table, the adult voices, into her own liquid space where all was fluid and floating free. She would stare at the back of someone's hat in church, and find herself swinging from dangly, satin ribbons through pitch black space. Or while watching someone's mouth move, she'd be creeping over big, molar-shaped rocks, sliding down into the jaws of a velvety cavern.

At first Cassiopeia had let herself be drawn into the heart of the Witness fold almost eagerly. There were baby showers and weddings and togetherness in abundance. But all the fun had conditions, and there was much to be relinquished: Easter bunnies, Santa Claus, and other "wordly" friends. Most of them had only a marginal existence for Cassiopeia anyway, but she wasn't sure about giving up the things she'd never had a chance at. And the Witness parties that replaced all this were always completely without surprise and imagination, two important, if virtually unknown, elements in Cassiopeia's world.

There was a veneer of superficiality that glossed over the Witness lives that Cassiopeia unknowingly reacted against, like a secret bitter taste that lingers long after the sweetness fades away. L.A. was all stucco, pink and aqua, and mica-flecked. Cassiopeia's only escape was a public pool where she floated anonymously on her turquoise air mattress, sick with worry that she was going to be made to go door to door with the Witnesses.

Her savior came in the form of a huge, pachyderm of a man named Milton Abrew. Eileen had met him at the Piggly Wiggly when she slipped in a pool of spilled Mazola oil and fell flat on her back. Milton, the store manager, drove her home that day and even made an appointment for Eileen to have her spine checked out, which somehow led to a dinner date. The Witnesses most surely did not approve of Milton Abrew. He was not one of them and, therefore, suspect. At first they took the soft approach, Larry Schram counseling Eileen gently about the dangers of worldy influences. But then came firmer talks, then warnings that were really threats in disguise.

One Sunday they were all sitting down to the big, mid-day meal that always followed church. Mrs. Schram had baked a chicken, and Larry was slicing it. It was the Witnesses' custom to have the children come up with their plates to be served, and Cassiopeia was the first in line. As his knife pierced a steaming thigh, a pale, wine-colored juice flowed out.

"MOTHER . . . We can't eat this chicken, this

chicken's not DONE!!!" Mr. Schram's voice graduated upwards as he threw down the carving knife in disgust.

The knife twirled once on the tablecloth, and then flipped off, planting itself straight into the top of Cassiopeia's bare foot. Blood spattered everywhere. Eileen tried to contain it with her napkin, unleashing a wild pack of cuss words, grown all the more vicious having been held captive so long.

As they sat waiting in the hospital emergency room, gauze wadded on Cassiopeia's foot, Eileen's face was a white mask, her pale eyes nearly disappearing as she tried to smile.

"You're being very brave about your foot," she said finally.

"Mom, will you promise me something?"

"Sure. What is it, little chap?"

"I won't have to go door to door with the Witnesses, will I? Please don't make me."

"No, you won't." Eileen said.

"Promise?"

"I promise."

Six stitches and eight hours later, they were back at the Schrams packing their things. The Witnesses were gone off to Sunday evening Fellowship. Eileen called Milt, who came to pick them up in his brand new Chevy Nova, and their Witnessing days were over.

Eileen said she would not live with Milt unless they were married, and so, one week later, a local Justice of the Peace performed a brief and colorless ceremony with Cassiopeia a reluctant witness of a different sort this time. They moved into Milt's one-bedroom house in Tujunga Canyon, a house with a front yard filled with crawly cacti and a fireplace with each brick painted a different color. At first Cassiopeia was so glad to have escaped the Witnesses that she didn't mind sleeping on the pull-out sofa. But after a few weeks, Eileen decided Cassiopeia should have her own room, and Milton got out his tool box and made a makeshift bed for her on the service porch.

This was her first, very own room, and she didn't really mind the washer and dryer squeezed in a corner or the fuse box over her bed. A broom closet was converted for her clothes. She stored her socks and underwear in little cubbyholes of the egg crates Milton brought home. She lined the walls with movie magazine cut-outs: teen idols whose names she didn't even know. She stood a cardboard cut-out of Arthur Godfrey up in the corner, having begged Milton to bring it home for her from the store. Later, Arthur was joined by Jerry Lewis and Art Linkletter. She hung up crepe paper pineapples and leis from a discarded Hawaiian display. But the final touch that completed the tropical potpourri look was a wall-sized poster of a cougar that she acquired by flirting shamelessly with a young, pimply salesman at the Mercury dealership two blocks from Milton's house.

Eileen dived into cooking and shopping, clipping coupons and recipes and lining the shelves with potted meat, canned tamales, fruit cocktail, Spam, and assorted canned vegetables. She filled the freezer with stacks of meat trays, ground beef, steaks, pork chops, all from the Piggly Wiggly — at a discount.

She kept a running account of her shelves and replaced every item as it was used, said it gave her a nice, comfy feeling. And Eileen amazed the clerks by adding the bill in her head and quoting the total before they had rung it up. For Cassiopeia's thirteenth birthday, Eileen baked a white, layer cake sprinkled with red hots, and gum drops, and Milton brought out a big, cutout of Desi Arnaz playing bongos while sitting on a box of Fab. Eileen had added the letters, U-L-O-U-S and 13 after the word FAB. After they had eaten cake and neopolitan ice cream, Eileen brought out a portable hifi with a big bow on top, and Milton produced a card with a dog on the front saying, "Have a Doggone Good Birthday!" and a five dollar bill folded neatly inside. The next day, Cassiopeia went down and bought three records, "You are My Special Angel," "You're Sixteen, You're Beautiful, and You're Mine," and an obscure calypso record on sale.

There had never been music in her life before, and Cassiopeia became obsessive now, putting on the calypso record first thing in the morning, a song that began with a sledge hammer drum beat that Eileen compared to Nazi storm troopers. Cassiopeia would try for the loudest possible volume first, knowing that Eileen would holler, "Turn that damn Nazi music down."

"You're Sixteen" got scratched when Eileen was pulling clothes from the washer and dropped a pile of wet towels on the record in the middle of the song. After that, it skipped on "and ooh, when we kissed, we could not stop," repeating "we could not stop" over and over until Eileen screamed or Cassiopeia got up and moved the needle. Cassiopeia took to squirreling away in her makeshift bedroom, playing her three records repeatedly, reading Trixie Belden and Nancy Drew mysteries, and lying on her bed, legs up in the air, twirling a battered old baton with her feet, a habit of both nervous and obsessive origins. Every so often the baton would thump to the floor, and Eileen would pound on the wall.

Cassiopeia had no friends. She was attending Mt. Whitney Junior High, which seemed like an enormous club she was never invited to join. Cassiopeia was too unhappy and shy to go up to anyone and easily sifted through the crowds, an untanned, skinny ghost. She watched with distant admiration a wishbone thin, Mexican girl with hair to her waist who seemed to be in on "the secret." It all seemed like some kind of initiation, with coded language that Cassiopeia was not privy to, and left her always with the "outside" feeling, both comfortable and awkward.

So Cassiopeia went from library to school to public pool to her bedroom, avoiding all unnecessary contact — a strange, scraggly phantom lost in the asphalt, pastel-hell heat and smog of L.A. However, with Milt and Eileen, things went from bored stalemate to outright war. It all began when Milton threw his back out trying to capture a sparrow that had flown into the Piggly Wiggly and was roosting on the open rafters. Milt took to his bed for two weeks, and then had to go on disability. The doctors gave conflicting diagnoses, and one even suggested surgery. After six weeks, and at Milt's suggestion, Eileen announced that she was going to work as a checker at the Piggly Wiggly. Milt's benefits were coming to an end, and he was still in too much pain to work. Every hour he was up cost him two hours in bed to recover.

Eileen left the house each morning now in a red smock with EILEEN embroidered on the pocket and returned at five, hot, frazzled, and cranky. They ate canned spaghetti, frozen pizza, or creamed tuna on toast, Milton taking his on a tray in front of the t.v. that had been set up for him on the bedroom dresser. Eileen's eyes turned a pale shade of yellow, and she developed a nagging cough. She seemed to be staring all the way to China, sitting silently for hours in an orange sling chair. Cassiopeia felt the storm long before it hit, like some kind of electrical pulse in the air or a high pressure zone (Eileen) meeting a low (Milton).

Eileen had thrown some clothes in the washer one Saturday and asked Cassiopeia if she wanted to go with her to the beauty parlor. Cassiopeia liked to read the movie magazines as she sat tucked between the soothing hum of the helmet dryers and the sweet indolence of shampoo and rinse smells. But Eileen had mixed the date up; her appointment was for the next week, and they had to turn around and go back home. Eileen was not happy, and Cassiopeia, sensing this, reacted by clumsily spilling peanuts all over the back steps on their way back in. Scooping up nuts, they could hear Milton on the phone. He obviously hadn't heard them. "

"Yea," he said, "I just may not go back to work . . . Got the old lady workin' now . . . I kinda like this stayin' home stuff . . . worked hard all my life . . ."

It was the beginning of their own personal cold war, with Cassiopeia struggling if not to maintain neutrality then to just stay out of the action. Eileen began by marching into the house and into Cassiopeia's bedroom, where she proceeded to remove Milt's wet underwear from the washer. She carried it to the bathroom, where she first dumped it onto the floor and then began flushing his briefs, one by one, down the toilet.

"Now you have a reason for staying home," she said, launching into one of her fits. She dismantled the living room in about five minutes flat. Milton was too surprised at first to react. In fact, a man of limited imagination, his best efforts to retaliate only produced long, chilly silences or brooding sessions on the back steps where he sat spitting tobacco and obscenities into the night. One chilly week later, Eileen got up from the sofa where she had been sleeping since the blow-up and clicked off the bowling tournament Milt had been watching on the t.v. in the bedroom.

"O.K." she said, "do you go back to work, or do I leave?"

Milt might have been unimaginative but he was not completely stupid, and he knew, or believed anyway, that Eileen had nowhere to go.

"Look here, I've been manager of that store for twenty-seven years now. That's half my life almost . . ."

"You're not in pain," Eileen snapped. "You've been faking it."

"Not all the time," said Milt lamely, losing ground.

"If I go, then you'll have to go back to work won't you?"

Milt sighed. "Just give me some time to get on my feet, woman. Have some heart." He was crumbling.

"O.K. You've got until Monday morning, eight

o'clock to get on your feet!" she said, slapping his white plastic loafers smartly onto the foot of the bed.

Monday morning, Milt called the Piggly Wiggly and found out he needed a doctor's excuse before returning to work. Eileen furiously buttoned her smock and left for work. When she came in at five, her first words to Milt were "So, when is your doctor's appointment?"

"Next week," he said, looking really scared. "It was the earliest I could get."

Eileen said nothing. She went to the kitchen and turned on the oven. She carefully washed two potatoes, speared them with nails, and popped them into the oven. She got out the cast iron skillet, placed it on the front burner and turned on the gas. Then she went to the refrigerator, took out a tray of thawed hamburger, and formed two patties, pressing them down into the cast iron skillet. She boiled two cobs of corn and laid out two plates on the table. When everything was done, she announced calmly and distinctly, "Cassiopeia, dinner is served."

Milt watched all this from behind an outdated *Newsweek* in the living room.

"How was school today?" Eileen asked, falsely cheerful, as they lifted their forks. This was only the beginning. The rest of the week, Eileen washed and dried only her own and Cassiopeia's clothes, cooked exactly six pancakes — three for each of them — for breakfast, two hot dogs for dinner, and made only her side of the bed. She baked a small lemon pie, Milt's favorite, and divided it in two equal half moons, carrying one half to Cassiopeia's room and eating the other herself in front of the t.v. with Milt watching. She washed her and Cassiopeia's dishes, left Milt's to crust in the sink. Milt alternated between having pizza or chicken dinners delivered, which Cassiopeia would rather have had although she didn't dare say so.

Milt ate loquats off the backyard tree for breakfast and cold, leftover pizza for lunch. He spent less time in bed now but spent most of the day reading the paper on a chaise longue in the backyard. The day of Milt's appointment with the doctor, Eileen worked a late shift. When she came in from work, Milt was still on his chaise, smoking in the dark. Eileen stopped on her way in and was there a long while, their voices woven into the chain-smoked night air. Cassiopeia searched Eileen's face when she came in, but it was flat with a bored-looking tiredness.

"Let's go for a walk on the hill, chap," said Eileen. Their street was at the bottom of a canyon and directly across the street, a hill covered with cactus, scrubby iceplant, and lifeless brush spiraled straight up. They started on a narrow path of switchbacks, zigzagging up the hill. They stopped at the top, breathless from exertion and from the sight of L.A. below them, the fan of lights sprayed out like a magician's rhinestone-studded cape. The scent of the cool air reminded Cassiopeia of driving at night, infecting her with an exotic desire that was exciting and new. An unusual spark of communion flew between her and Eileen. Most of the time, Cassiopeia took no more notice of Eileen than of the water or electricity. It was there. You turned a tap, flipped a switch, and the need was met. And Eileen returned the favor, washing and folding

Cassiopeia's clothes, leaving sandwiches and chips on the washer for her, — bandaging, delivering, grooming, asking little in return.

Eileen's fits, her bent for wandering, and her blind adaptability all interfered with real closeness. The only person ever to really break through was Juanita. Eileen looked up at the stars.

"There's one up there with your name, huh chap?"

"There's a whole constellation," Cassiopeia thought, but didn't say it, afraid to break the spell. She thought of taking hold of Eileen's hand, like she had when she was little, but felt too foolish to actually do it.

"I guess we can't see the stars too good for all these other lights." Eileen said.

"Yea, I guess not," answered Cassiopeia, thinking, "They're like fake stars, drowning out the real ones." She was aware then of more than just their cold beauty. She felt spaces in herself, like the spaces between the stars that the constellation charts showed, like the dots she traced lines between as a child, completing the dancing dog, the birthday cake with lighted candles, the fenced yard and house that *could* be hers someday. But not now.

Eileen's heavy sigh drifted into the night. "Guess it's time for us to be moving on, old chap."

Cassiopeia didn't move, didn't respond. Eileen waited a long time, then, "Imagine . . . that man thought I was going to support him for the rest of his life."

"Well," Cassiopeia thought, "didn't you think the same thing? He just beat you to it, playing your own game." But she knew better than to say it and looked away from Eileen's deserted eyes wet with the lights of dying stars.

Eileen left a note for Milton:

> I'm entitled to half of everything.
> I'll settle for the bonds and the savings account. The lawyer will be calling you.
>
> Eileen
>
> P.S. The checking is overdrawn.

Chapter 13
•
Fresno, California

The first evening star bloomed in a heavy coral dusk. Cassiopeia rattled the ice in her wine cooler. Aside from her one trip through the park and to the library, she had sat in the overgrown yard for most of a week now just dreaming, thinking, reminiscing, a stack of library books piled beside her on the wooden spool table: *Your World Through Astronomy*, *The Complete Herb Book*, *The Disappearing Amazon*, *World Treasury of Insects in Color*, *The Photographer's Eye*, *The Oceans*. She had picked up one after another, sampling the contents: maps of star clusters; meadowsweet, valerian, herbal remedies of the Indians; oceanic paths of the tides connected to the sun and the moon; Amazon Indians living outside of time; how a photo is "a secret about a secret." She had even read about her own constellation, Cassiopeia: "A small but unmistakable constellation, its five brightest stars forming a conspicuous M or W near the north pole."

The coral sky faded away to the pale sheen of polished pewter then seemed to tarnish before her eyes with the failing light. Cassiopeia felt the wind steeping in her blood, the weight of dusk gathering in her limbs. As darkness emptied down, the neighbors scraped lawn chairs on their patio, scraps of laughter and conversation spilling over the fence. A man's voice said, "C'mon, Carol, tell me. It's not fair." Whether Carol answered fairly or not, Cassiopeia couldn't tell, Carol's answer lost in the choke of wisteria and darkness. Then she heard the low murmuring and combined laughter of lovers who know the night will soothe and join their mutual aches.

Cassiopeia went into the kitchen and poured another wine cooler. Even the name was appealing after the heat of the day. She had napped most of the afternoon and now felt wide-eyed and gregarious, but even Zona's cat, Mooshie, was lying low.

It felt strange to have this time to herself alone. She had called Marie that morning, thinking maybe they could go to a movie or something, but Marie had family visiting all week. Two wine coolers later, she dialed Hap's work number, not sure why or what she'd say. There was a chance he was working late. She never called his home. Three rings and the message machine came on. She hesitated, feeling awkward and wine-mulled.

"Hi, Hap This is Cassiopeia. If you still want to talk to me, my number is 224-8906. It would be nice to hear from you. That's all." She hung up, half sorry she'd rung.

No sooner had she settled herself in the yard with the crickets than the phone began to ring. She headed for the house with no particular haste and stared through three rings before answering.

"Cassie, this is Hap. Where you been? I called pretty near every motel in Fresno trying to find you. Why didn't you call before?"

Hap didn't seem to have considered that maybe she hadn't wanted to contact him. She felt foolish and tongue-tied now, not having thought out what she'd say, and the wine made her head feel fuzzy.

"I had to send Hope off to her godmother's," she blurted out.

"Well, she's O.K. isn't she?"

"Yes, but . . ."

"Look, Cassie, I'm coming to Fresno to see you." It was a statement, not a question, and Cassiopeia was beginning to regret making the call. She knew it would be useless to argue with Hap. From the beginning, he had paid her way. Therefore, he was in charge, and she had played it his way. Money, the great unequalizer, always served Hap well.

When Cassiopeia hung up the phone, she went back to her chair in the yard considerably sobered. "Dammit" she said to the moon, a finger away from full, and dangling low in the black sky. "Now what have I gone and done?"

It would have been so much easier if she'd just done nothing. Now she would have to make a decision. She heard a sprinkler's swish from nearby and the music of crickets from Carol's patio. She went to bed and tossed on a restless sea, landing a huge fish in her tiny boat. Its raw, purple gills open to the poisonous air, the fish thrashed in the boat as she tried to wrestle it down. She felt it around her, choking while the boat jerked and swayed.

In the morning, she woke later than usual. Hap was coming at five. "O.K." she thought, "I will just see how I feel. Maybe we'll have a good time. Maybe it's really right after all."

It was always tempting for her to think of Hap as "the answer." She spent the day cleaning Zona's tiny house and making a quick trip to the store. All week, she had done almost nothing, sitting in the straw chair looking at library books and letting her mind ramble at will through the universe. She took a shower and dressed. She had little to choose from. All she owned were jeans and t-shirts with a sprinkling of rhinestone stars and *The Satellite Lounge* in orbit on her chest. Dangling, silver-plated UFO earrings completed the costume. Bud had wanted them to wear silver high heels, but Marie had put her sensible bartender's foot down.

Cassiopeia opened Zona's closet and flipped through wild, floral mumus and outdated polyesters. She found one black sheath which was really too big, but belted it in and dug up a pair of not too gaudy earrings. All she needed now were shoes. Finally, with a sigh, she pulled out the silver heels she'd worn only once to work. Cassiopeia pulled her long, thick almond hair back in clips, gave her nose a swipe of make-up. She knew she was not beautiful, yet men often found her attractive and irrestible enough.

Hap arrived late — beyond his control, he said, but he didn't elaborate. He looked good. He had dropped about twenty pounds and added a caramel tan that Cassiopeia figured must be commercial since Hap was given to burning and peeling.

"You look great!" he said. He kissed her lightly and sank down onto the couch, feet stretched out, arms propped behind his head. "Whew! It's been a helluva day. Appointments clear up till this afternoon."

He looked around at the distress sale furniture and tacky knick-knacks. "Place sure is small. You here by yourself?"

He did not sound nearly so brash now as he had on the phone. Cassiopeia told him about Zona while she fixed herself a wine cooler and opened a Dos Equis for Hap.

"X marks the spot! Muy Bueno, Cassie. You remembered." He was smiling, and she noticed he wasn't wearing his usually crooked glasses.

"Where's your glasses?" she asked.

"Oh, I got contacts," he said, and then very quickly, "Hey, let's get something to eat."

Hap had a new car, something silver and low, tapered like a bullet. When Cassiopeia shut the door, it was like settling into a new leather womb. Hap selected buttons, in full control of lights, air, sound; a self-contained atmosphere. One of the buttons triggered the stereo and "Mountain of Love" poured out. Cassiopeia looked quickly at Hap, who looked back and winked. Hap was a master in the game of contrivance. He was also a gambler and strategist. There were those who called him ruthless, but Hap said he just liked to win. Assessing her wariness on the phone, he had plotted his moves carefully, opening with a cool detachment so as not to scare her off.

But he had tipped his hand with "Mountain of Love," their old song. Cassie could see it now. He was out to win her back. Any reluctance she might show would only make him all the more determined. She was not surprised when he didn't ask her where she'd like to eat and pulled up at an expensive resaurant. All through dinner, Hap moved light and easy. He asked about Hope, shuffling smoothly forward and back in a calculated conversational choreography, but strangely made no mention of Cassiopeia's search for Ned.

He said he had a surprise and ordered champagne. When it came, they raised their glasses, and Hap said, "Let's drink to the future, Cassie. You may just be toasting the next mayor of Bakersfield."

His fake, tanned grin was everywhere. This was not at all what Cassiopeia expected. "What do you mean?" She fumbled, the effervescence moving buoyantly through her, straight to her head.

"Well, I've been building my political support for some time, and not long ago I was contacted by a whole group of oil company people who want me to be their man."

Cassiopeia raised her glass again. "Here's to your success, Hap," she said, feeling completely confused. Why would he want to win her back now? Surely she'd just be in the way. Surely he wasn't still planning on divorcing his wife and marrying her, not in the middle of a mayoral campaign. "He must think he can keep me on the side indefinitely," she thought. They hadn't discussed where he'd stay that night yet. She had planned to settle that right away, but hadn't had the nerve to bring it up. Now, she felt angry and reckless. "Where are you staying tonight?" she blurted out.

"Well, I'd just counted on your hospitality, I

guess." He looked hurt.

"I'm surprised to hear that after you saw my small place," she countered.

"You know," he said, "I don't think you're glad I'm running for mayor."

"Don't be silly. Why should I care? And that's got nothing to do with the size of my bed either."

"I'll get a motel then," he said, retreating. Then, after an uneasy lull, "Hey, Cassie. This is no good. We're having a reunion. I have an idea. Let's go dancing, have some fun."

"I don't think so." Cassiopeia didn't like the way she was feeling. She hadn't planned on having an emotional reaction.

"O.K. Cassie, what's going on? I just want things to be the way they were before."

Cassiopeia started to say, "But the way things were before was only temporary." She stopped. Hap had maneuvered her into advocating for something she wasn't even sure she wanted. How did she ever imagine she could play his game and not lose?

"O.K." she said, "let's go dancing. I want some more champagne too." She felt like she was drowning; the harder she struggled, the worse it would be. No one spoke in the car's cool trajectory. Hap's taste for expensive restaurants did not extend to night clubs. He pulled up at The Tenderfoot Club, a country-western/top ten dive. This place did not even pretend elegance; no restraint had been wasted on decor, wrought iron and veined mirrors galore. It was Friday night, and the place was crowded with hard hat cowboys and secretaries who used party only as a verb.

The only table they could find was right in front
of the band. Hap ordered the champagne and the waitress laughed in his face. "You're too far west in this
town to get champagne, cowboy," she said. Hap settled
for a Dos Equis and Cassiopeia ordered a whiskey
sour. She thought how often she had envied her customers at work, their absorption in themselves and
complete indifference to her.

The band was jerking through a sloppy version
of "Kansas City." The girl singer rocked on spiked heels.
She was thin as the microphone stand she appeared to
be strangling and looked somehow familiar. Cassiopeia
stared. It was Ned's girl, the one with the cat named
Chop Suey. She had done something to her hair,
changed the color. It was all streaked and swept to the
side. She had on a low-cut dress with long, silver
sleeves, and a skirt slit up to her thigh. The dress was
all spangley, and Cassiopeia thought she looked like a
shiny fishing lure as she jiggled through "Kansas City."
Her voice was surprisingly good, rather low and dusky.
"Gonna slow it down some now," she breathed into the
mike. Hap pulled Cassiopeia up and onto the dance
floor. He was not a good dancer, but he led exception-
ally well. She felt propped in his arms as they twirled on
the saucer-shaped dance floor. Cassiopeia felt as if she
were trapped inside a kaleidoscope. Reflections and
refractions of herself and Hap shattered with every
turn. When they sat down, she felt as if her stomach
still spun.

"Hap, I don't feel so good. I'll be back in a
minute or two." She headed for the ladies room. "That's
what I get for a second night of drinking," she thought.

The bathroom reeked an industrial unpleasant-
ness, but at least there was a chair and she sat down,
feeling a dark surge of nausea. She dug in her purse
and found a soda cracker wrapped in cellophane. Her
face in the mirror stared back, pale and foreign-looking.
About ten minutes later, she felt a little better, and
stood up shakily, thinking she'd go back and order a
club soda. When Cassiopeia came out of the ladies
room, the room was saturated with blue layers of
smoke. She had stopped to get her bearings and look
for their table when she felt a hand gripping her arm. It
was the skinny girl singer. The band was on a break.
"Aren't you with that man in front of the bandstand?"
she asked urgently.

"Uh . . . yes, why?"

"Hey, honey, I wouldn't go back there if I was
you. Look over there now." Cassiopeia strained to see
through the tangle of people and smoke. A peroxide
blonde who looked a lot like Hap was sitting in
Cassiopeia's chair and glaring at Hap, who was chatter-
ing, moving his hands like a frantic deaf mute. They
were arguing, and Hap pulled something small and
white out of his wallet and jabbed it repeatedly. "

"She's hot as a thirty-eight. I couldn't help over-
hearing her say she was his wife and ask him where the
bitch was. Said she was gonna tear her into little,
cheap, floozy pieces."

Cassiopeia froze. "What should I do?"

"Follow me." The girl led her through the back
tables, down a narrow, black hallway, through another
door, into a storage room stacked with chairs and
boxes labeled Seagrams and Budweiser, and out anoth-

er door into the parking lot. "See that bank over there? Wait right by the bushes. I'll call you a taxi."

"Are you sure this is necessary? Maybe I should tell Hap . . ."

"Look honey, I saw a woman's nose ripped off here once. Another jealous woman shoved her so hard from behind, her face slammed into the dance floor. Took forty some stitches to get it back on. It was a bloodbath too . . . ruined my silver stretch pants."

"I really appreciate your helping me," Cassiopeia stammered, embarrassed.

"Forget it," the girl said, turning to shut the door. Then she stuck her head back out. "Look honey, why don't you get yourself a job in a nice, quiet library somewhere?"

The door shut with a gust. Cassiopeia ran to the shadows of the bushes by the bank, trying to conceal herself in the shrubbery. She heard voices from the Tenderfoot Club. Two women ran to their car, laughing shrilly. "Did you see that cowboy nerd? He was staring so hard I thought he'd pop an eyeball. Let's go . . . to The Sundowner." They peeled out of the parking lot.

At least five more minutes elapsed, then Cassiopeia heard Hap's voice bursting out the door. "God dammit, B.J. I told you there's no broad. I don't know what you thought you saw. And I don't like you having me tailed, either."

"Why would you come to a place like this by yourself? I know she's here, and Paul saw someone in the car with you. This ain't the end of it, Mr. Wanna Be Mayor!"

At this moment, Cassiopeia saw the checkered

cab pull up slowly, creeping down the driveway between the Tenderfoot Club and the bank. The driver was cruising, scanning slowly for his fare. Hap saw the cab and must have figured it out. He tried to take his wife's arm and lead her to the car, but not before Cassiopeia stepped out of the bushes and signaled to the driver. Both Hap's head and his wife's head swivelled in her direction. All three sets of eyes met. Cassiopeia raised her hand in that half-second, blew them both a kiss and jumped in the cab.

"Fast," she said, pointing straight ahead. The cab driver stepped on the gas. Cassiopeia looked back and saw Hap's arms raised in self-defense against the flash of his wife's pearly cocktail purse.

"Looks like you got out just in time," the cabbie said.

"In more ways than one," replied Cassiopeia. It took all her cash to pay the cab fare. Strangely enough, when she got home, she felt starved. All she could find was a box of Captain Crunch, and she poured out a huge bowl and ate greedily, dribbling milk down her chin. Then she lay on her bed in the dark, fully clothed, her silver heels pointing to the night sky like two beached fish whose scales flashed moonlight.

The room seemed dipped in heavy cream. The clock spoke its one dependable syllable. A dog barked to hear itself bark. Cassiopeia closed her eyes but did not sleep. Her dress was very warm and close. With the toe of her shoe, she punched the button of the fan, heard the blades purring through the air. Lulled by the sound, she watched its arms sweeping moonlight about the room, a shadowy dervish whirling his scarves.

Wildly, her eyes cast about the room, found only a two foot tall Galliano bottle with a soldier in a tall, plume hat on the front. Zona had filled it with water and a drop of lavender ink. Other bottles, all in various curvaceous shapes, she'd filled with different shades of blue and violet, edging the windows to bend the morning light. With night, the inky liquids darkened, like deeper fathoms of the sea. Cassiopeia felt herself sinking, descending into mysterious leagues where lonely, aqueous eyes circled the depths of her. She wanted to kick out and paddle up, surface thousands of miles away near warmer regions of light, but an immense, oceanic weight held her down. If she could only move her legs, but they were useless blobs, two still lumps like netted fish. She tried to move her arms, but they had been removed, and there she lay, barely breathing, stupified and paraplegic in the darkness.

Chapter 14
Chevyville, Illinois

"Fish or cut bait." It was one of Eileen's favorite sayings, and once again she and Cassiopeia were cutting bait, headed back to Chevyville. Eileen had tried to call Juanita and, getting no answer, decided to surprise her. Eileen knew Juanita could be flighty. She was always there for you, as long as she was there. Trouble was, there could be anywhere.

Cassiopeia didn't like it, and begged Eileen not to leave L.A. until reaching Juanita, but Eileen, fearing a hassle from Milton, was ready to roll. And so they rolled . . . out into the dazzle of L.A. lights on the midnight Greyhound express to Chicago. From there, they took a local to Moline where, three days after leaving L.A., Eileen went straight to a pay phone and dialed Juanita at 5:30 in the morning.

Cassiopeia, watching the bruised edge of sky fading to silver light, sat on the scuffed suitcases that once again contained the accumulated sum of their scattered lives. She had been forced to leave behind her *Teen Rave* and *Tiger Beat* magazines, her record player, her baton, and, almost, her wall-sized poster of a growling cougar's face. To each item that she'd moaned and stomped over, Eileen had said the same thing:

"Give it up kid. We'll get a brand new one when we get to Chevyville." Eileen was making her own wrenching sacrifices: a carved ivory dresser set, a complete line of Vivian Woodard cosmetics, a lighted dressing table mirror just like the stars', a floor-length quilted satin peignoir, and, worst of all, a pair of peau de soie Springalators with rhinestone studded heels.

They had crammed four of their biggest suitcases full to the bursting point, and at the last minute Eileen pulled out a handful of underwear and stuck in the rhinestone heels. "I can always buy new panties," she explained.

Without saying a word, Cassiopeia pulled down her poster, folded it up, and fitted it in the place of her own wad of underwear.

In the phone booth, Eileen had turned her back to Cassiopeia — not a good sign. She'd dialed twice, and now it was obvious no one was answering. Cassiopeia was not one to panic, but her face was now caved in with fear. This was straight out of her nightmares. Never having a stable home base, she'd never internalized home, making her especially vulnerable to unsettledness. Eileen came out of the booth. "Let's go get breakfast," she said, ignoring Cassiopeia's scared, indicting eyes.

In the plastic booth of Flo's Cafe, Eileen smoked, watching Cassiopeia devour a stack of pancakes soaked in purple syrup. "Look, I know you're worried, but it WILL be O.K. Juanita doesn't stay gone that long. And anyway, we're rolling in dough, kid. We could even stay in a hotel."

Cassiopeia watched in amazement as Eileen flashed a Diner's Club card onto the little tray with the bill. So that explained why Eileen had encouraged her to splurge on breakfast. "Milton owes me a few, I think," she said, fixing her mouth in her gold compact mirror. It wasn't exactly true that they were rolling in dough, but for them, used to living precariously at best, things were on the up side. After breakfast, Eileen went to the pay phone on the corner. Cassiopeia could see her in the booth from the smeary cafe window. The bottom of her cocoa was gritty and sweet. She swallowed it just as Eileen returned, out of luck again.

"What do we do now?" Cassiopeia's face said, "This better be good."

"Only one thing to do . . ." Eileen paused dramatically. "We go to the movies." It was a double feature, and they saw it twice, after having taken a taxi back to the bus depot to check their bags and walking around until twelve, when the matinees started.

They emerged from the theater, bleary eyed and stiff. Cassiopeia felt slightly nauseous, but Eileen dismissed it as too much sugar and junk, since they'd lunched on Jujubes, Milk Duds, and popcorn in the theater. It was after six. The sky was filling with dark, purplish clumps of clouds and the air held a late, summer chill. Cassiopeia leaned wearily against the telephone booth as Eileen dialed with a bright red fingernail.

Eileen's smugness about reaching Juanita was starting to get to her. She almost didn't want Juanita to answer, just to prove Eileen wrong. Suddenly Eileen thumped on the glass, and mouthed the word, "Bingo!"

and made the A-O.K. sign. Her words were too muffled for Cassiopeia to catch, but Eileen seemed subdued. There was usually a lot of laughing and joking with Juanita. Eileen was on the phone for about five minutes before hanging up.

"A car's coming for us in about a half-hour, or so," she said. "Are you hungry?"

Eileen was already headed over to Flo's Cafe. Cassiopeia ran to catch up with her. They sat down in their same booth, and Eileen ordered a steak sandwich. Cassiopeia ordered a hamburger and fries. About an hour later, when Cassiopeia was pushing the last of her fries through a puddle of ketchup, Eileen signaled for the check. A Dodge station wagon, the color of a smoggy sky, had pulled up in front of Flo's. Hurriedly, they paid the bill and went outside, but it wasn't Juanita's laughing mule face Cassiopeia saw. A plump freckled woman, with the face of an eight year old girl was at the wheel. She jumped out and shyly reached to hug Eileen, who was a reluctant hugger.

"Hello, Eileen. I remember you, Cassiopeia," she said as she turned to her. A sweet tenderness laced the woman's voice voice when she said her name. "And Juanita goes on about Cassiopeia all the time." She paused as if she'd run out of words.

"Who are you?" Cassiopeia blushed, realizing how awkward that sounded.

"I'm sorry. I'm Lily, a friend of Juanita's." She looked at Eileen somewhat puzzled, as if wondering why Cassiopeia hadn't been filled in. But Cassiopeia was used to this.

"So Juanita's not home?" There was accusation

in her voice.

"Shall we get in the car?" Eileen said, somewhat impatiently. "We need to stop by the Greyhound station, Lily, to get our bags."

When they were in the car finally and headed out of Moline, Cassiopeia broached the subject of Juanita again.

"Well, she went on this spur-of-the-moment vacation. She got an offer to go stay in a cabin on Lake Michigan, up north of Chicago. Real nice, it sounded. She called me Sunday night. Said she'd only planned to stay the week-end but then decided to stay on some more. I'm sure glad you caught me, Eileen. I've just been going over to feed the cats and water the plants."

"I tried calling her Friday night," Eileen said, "Line was busy from eleven till two — a.m., that is — and then there was no answer."

"Well . . ." Cassiopeia had the feeling Lily measured her words for her benefit. "She took off Friday night right about two in the morning, I think. It was spur-of-the-moment, like I said."

Eileen was silent. Cassiopeia watched the telephone wires dotted with perching birds dissecting the distance they plowed through, the wide green swath of trees, the corridor of silken corn that bent and whispered to her as they passed. Something rose inside, a sourness that spilled upward. Her head throbbed, and she slumped over in the back seat.

Lily finally broke the awkward silence. "I can't believe how much Cassie has grown."

"She's getting to be a young lady, I guess, but she's still a little girl inside." Cassiopeia hated it when

Eileen discussed her "maturing process." It did not seem to matter whether Cassiopeia was present or not.

"It's not easy on any of us," Lily said.

They lowered their voices then, but Cassiopeia could hear if she lay very still. They were discussing someone named Jack. "He's how old?" she heard Eileen say. Then, "She should know better . . ."

Straining to listen, Cassiopeia fit the pieces together. Juanita had met a young man at the filling station where she'd taken her Mercury to have the oil changed and the tires rotated. When she picked it up, she'd gotten to talking to the new mechanic. Next thing they were having a drink. Then he came over to her place, which explained the busy signal — telephone taken off the hook. And next thing anyone knew, they'd taken off at two in the morning for his brother's cabin up by Lake Michigan.

"I just hope she doesn't make too big a fool of herself."

Lily was less judgmental. "At least let's hope she's havin' fun if she does."

Cassiopeia drifted into a feverish, restless sleep then, dreaming of riding a snow-white stallion across a blistering desert so hot the wind burned her face and singed her mouth dry. A dark man on a dark horse would draw up beside her and then drop back. She could not see his face but felt an ominousness that circled near. She rode faster, as if to outrun this dark force, but got nowhere. Then she remembered she could fly and stood up on the horse's back and kicked off and up into the starry night's desert sky. A dome of stars spun around her as she flew, cool and exhilarated.

She woke clammy and weak in a dim and unfamiliar room. She could hear other voices now and occasional laughter, the clink of ice cubes. She saw lazy smoke drifting in from someone's cigarette. She heard the deep rumble of a man's laughter. Cassiopeia sat up. Jack and Juanita!

She crept from bed and peeked through the crack of the door. Juanita sat on a man's lap at the table. He wasn't much bigger than she. She blocked his face, but as Juanita leaned forward to tamp out her cigarette, Cassiopeia got a good view of him. She gasped. He was black. Then looking closer she saw that he wasn't exactly black. No. He had pretty light skin, sort of olive, but kinky black hair that bushed around his head and became a soft looking beard and mustache. He reminded Cassiopeia of one of the Smith Brothers on the cough drop box.

Juanita was trying to talk Eileen into something. Cassiopeia put her ear to the crack of the door. Juanita wanted Eileen to go back to the cabin with them for a couple of days more. "We got it till Friday, girl . . . C'mon . . . Sure . . . Cassie will be all right. Lily's offered to stay with her. It's just the flu. How often you get to have any fun, girl? And frying bacon in the nude don't, count."

Everyone laughed. "She's fourteen . . . C'mon, Eileen . . ." Juanita could be very persuasive, especially with Eileen.

"See, this is how she talked me into going to Russell's funeral . . ."

"That ain't true. You wanted to go much as I did. Lord! I'll bet he was a beautiful corpse . . . just as pretty as if he'd been homecoming king."

"Well, let me go see how she is . . ."

Cassiopeia leaped back under the quilt just as Eileen came tiptoeing in. "Cassie, you awake? Hon, how you feeling?"

Cassiopeia turned over and said weakly, "Better, I guess . . . Stomach's better anyway."

Eileen put her palm on Cassiopeia's forehead, surprising her with its firm warmth. "Fever's gone down. Juanita's here with her friend, Jack. Honey, they want me to go back to the cabin for a few days with them. How would you feel about that?"

Cassiopeia wasn't sure how she felt. She was not used to being fussed over, even when she was sick, and being an undemanding child anyway, Cassiopeia had gotten by with Eileen's sustenance level of nurturing. But now, she was entering a new phase. The first rumblings of adolescence were being heard. She needed more right now and didn't know it, but she paid for her unawareness with an arsenal of volcanic emotions that could erupt at any time.

"Oh sure, go on Mama. I'll be O.K. I'm feeling better, lots better."

And so they took off in the middle of the night again, like carefree vagabonds. Juanita came in before they left and smothered Cassiopeia with kisses and promises.

When Cassiopeia woke in the morning, she could not place herself. She thought she was in a motel at first but then realized it was someone's house. Whose? She heard an unfamiliar humming nearby in the kitchen.

"What if I have woken from a dream in someone else's life? Could this be a dream?" She touched her arm, and its solidity reassured her. It must have been the flu that caused her prolonged state of confusion. Wobbling, she walked over to the dresser and saw her pale, lost face floating up in the mirror like the ghost of a moon. Then she remembered where she was but couldn't shake the sense of strangeness.

She took up Juanita's face powder and patted over the contours of her face, drew bright peach lips over her own, and rubbed purple onto her eyelids. She looked down. She'd had the same jeans and t-shirt on for days now. She pulled out her suitcase and rummaged through the jumble of clothes. She took out a pair of panties, a grayish bra, her only other good pair of jeans, and a pale blue, button-down collar shirt. Lily was at the stove when Cassiopeia came in.

"Do you think you could eat some cream of wheat?" she asked shyly. She seemed happy as she bustled around the kitchen.

"O.K. maybe a little. But could I get a bath first?" Then she added "Please."

"Oh sure honey. I shoulda thought of it." And Lily raced around pulling out towels and running a bath. "It's always a good sign when you feel like a bath."

When they both sat down to the table, Cassie saw that Lily had covered their bowls with pot lids. "Just like the hospital," she said. There was a stack of toast, "Unbuttered, so it won't upset your tummy," and a pot of peppermint tea.

"Thanks," Cassiopeia smiled weakly and tried to eat, still not sure about food going in. "Mmmm. Good."

Cassiopeia wasn't much good at conversation with strangers. "Tastes different from my mom's; hers has lumps."

Lily was making her nervous, watching her eat, silent, just smiling. In L.A. ,Cassiopeia had gotten used to eating her meals alone in her tiny room, on a t.v. tray much of the time, or sitting at the table with Eileen while she fumed silently at Milt.

"Where do you live?" Cassiopeia asked to make conversation.

"Oh, it's not far from here. In fact, if you feel good enough, we could go over there today. I really do need to do some garden work."

"That'd be great," Cassiopeia was feeling weird and only semi-connected, like an astronaut tethered in space. There was something she was missing, but she wasn't able to identify what it was.

"Are you sure you feel like it?"

"Sure, I'm sure. I feel lots better. Lots."

Lily's was an old house with a wide porch set among massive pecan and chestnut trees and closely clipped lawns. The house sat on a large, well-trimmed and cared for half-acre lot toward the edge of town. Lily's two youngest children were still at their grandma's in Ohio. The oldest girl was getting settled for college.

"I don't do all this by myself." Lily waved over the serene lawn. "I get some help in, especially with the pruning. Except with the roses. They're my babies."

Lily set her up on a chaise longue in the back yard under a huge shade tree. She gave Cassiopeia a stack of her old *Ladies Home Journals*, movie magazines that belonged to her daughters, and a pot of tea. Cassiopeia looked up from the slick revelations of Debbie and Eddie and Natalie to a mass of red, late roses that burst over the hedges and climbed along arched trellises.

Lily was pulling out dead tomato vines and stacking them in a pile, a few red-orange globes still clinging. Some late red peppers gleamed waxily proud and sensuous against the fence. Chrysanthemum buds had begun to open, and everywhere color exploded against the velvety green.

Cassiopeia sipped her tea and watched Lily snipping, raking, and pulling out things that had "seen their day." Part of her wanted to climb a vine and swing and part of her wanted to paint her lips and kiss the wind. Cassiopeia stood up. "

Where's the bathroom? I think I've had too much tea."

Inside, Cassiopeia passed the photographs that lined the mantle: somber, crew-cut boys and the oldest girl in her graduation hairdo and draped velvet. She had Lily's baby face. Cassiopeia sat on the toilet and studied the turquoise and black tile fanned in rows of diamonds. The toilet paper was all gone, and she looked around and found an extra roll under a little turquoise crocheted cap on the tank behind her. Then she looked down and saw the toilet paper's bright red smear. It was blood, and it had come from her. She felt herself and nothing felt different. It could be her period, she thought, or it could be from being sick, something torn loose inside. She wiped again, and there was another reddish streak. Then she began to sob, and the tears spilled out so quickly, she had no time to consider why.

Lily had come in the house and was knocking softly on the door. "Cassie, hon. What is it? Are you sick again?" Cassiopeia pulled up her pants and opened the door a crack. She just stood there with the tears between them.

"Can I come in?" Lily's worried eyes were deepening to alarm. Cassiopeia wanted to stop crying, but the spillway was open, her whole body enslaved to this one function. Without a word, Lily held her then, and as she did so, she spotted the pinkish-red tinge in the toilet bowl, and she knew. They stood in the bathroom with Lily's arms around her for an immeasurable time, a space between breath held and never let out. It was Alice time, when she drowned in the pool of tears, the clock on the other side of the looking glass.

Cassiopeia had spent the whole eighth grade in torture because of her body's betrayal, sure that she alone lacked the necessary equipment for womanhood. She had watched every girl in her class initiated and waited and waited, and then decided she was singled out for this stigma. One night, she had cried herself to sleep thinking of the complete physical failure of her body in a realm so natural and accessible to others. And now she was crying because it had happened. Eileen had never talked to her about the whole business but had found a little pamphlet she'd brought home from school called "Now You're a Lady." There was a belt and a napkin in an envelope that said "Compliments of Modess."

"Oh good," Eileen had said, "you know about

this. We'll put these away for you in the bathroom cabinet."

That had been all. Lily just let Cassiopeia cry now and after awhile she was done, and Lily pointed to the front of her blouse. "Look, you've soaked me clear through," she said as she handed her a Kleenex. "It's perfectly natural, you know." She rummaged through cabinets looking for a Kotex. "I hope you weren't afraid something was wrong, honey."

"I thought I might be torn inside because I've been sick." Cassiopeia would never have told Eileen this.

"It scared me, too, when it first happened to me. I thought I had cancer. But it's just a sign of change, honey. A beautiful change," she added. "Well," said Lily, rising, "I can't seem to find any Kotex. I'll just run to the store and get you some. Will you be O.K. by yourself?" Cassiopeia nodded yes. "I know. Just lie down on my bed and rest till I get back."

She led Cassiopeia into a cool, sparse room washed with leafy light. Cassiopeia laid down on the spread, a liquid green as silken as a body of water, and closed her eyes, floating on the lapping waves.

"I'll be right back," Lily called out as the door slammed.

The room smelled like roses and soap. Cassiopeia rolled on her side facing the window and watched the leaf patterns tumble on the wall. She pulled her legs up to her chest and drifted in between shadows and light. She must have slept, and when she next opened her eyes, she felt the bed dip just slightly. She turned over, and squinted up into a red-faced, puffy man, who was smiling in a funny way. He tried to laugh, but it turned into a groaning snort. Cassiopeia sat up just as he belly flopped onto the bed.

"Are you ready for me Rosie?" Blindly he grabbed her leg and held on, like it was keeping him afloat.

Cassiopeia wrenched away, but he was surprisingly strong for being as drunk as he was, and her struggle seemed to incite him to press harder. She flailed at his hands, which were now all over her.

"Come on Rosie. Don't fight me like this." His words spilled out sloppily.

"Get off her, you pig! Less you want me to cripple you where it counts." Lily was there in the doorway and moving closer. She had a squarish kind of gun, shakily pointed at his crotch. He didn't seem afraid at all, even when she cocked the trigger, but he did let go of Cassiopeia, and she dived off the bed.

"Oh, Rosie, why you so mean?"

Years later Cassiopeia would remember Lily with the gun, a look in her summer blue eyes of pure, cold resolve. The bed shook, and Cassiopeia saw as she stood up that he was laughing with his hand over his mouth like a child. He belched loudly once, groaned, "Ahhhh . . . Rosie . . ." rolled over again and began to snore.

Lily lowered the gun and later Cassiopeia would try, unsuccessfully, to remember what she'd done with it. The room rocked in its greenish shadows. The man was Lester, Lily's husband, and his soft blubbery snoring was now absorbed in the calm that had returned to the room.

Lily took Cassiopeia back to Juanita's in silent awkwardness. When they got there, she turned in the driver's seat. "I'm so sorry that happened. He's a very sick man, honey, and he mistook you for someone else."

Cassiopeia didn't have the nerve to ask the questions she wanted to ask: How long had he been like that? Was he being treated if he was sick? Had he done things like that before? Why did Lily put up with him? Instead she just said, "Does he still live there?"

"Yes . . ."

A terrible sadness crept into Lily's eyes. "Tomorrow, he'll start reforming. Usually he's harmless, really. He hasn't pulled anything like that in years. He's usually at work now. Must have gotten off early."

"Who's Rosie?"

"I don't know. But you are O.K., aren't you?"

"Yes, I"m O.K. He just . . ." she paused, "tried to grab me, that's all."

"That's bad enough. I feel like I didn't take very good care of you." Cassiopeia did not want Lily to blame herself.

"You did, really you did. Is that your gun?"

"It's his. He had it in the service, and I keep it hidden from him. I wouldn't have let him hurt you. You do know that, don't you?"

"I know it." Cassiopeia said, and she did. She'd heard the click of the trigger. And thus sealed an unspoken pact of silence between Lily, who did not ask it of her, and Cassiopeia, who never told Eileen or Juanita. It was one of many secrets to come between Cassiopeia and Eileen, but Cassie had no way of knowing the secrets had started long ago, even before her birth. Lily's secret also stretched out into the past, and if she had known how to unravel the tangled threads of *why* and *how*, to separate the *then* from *now*, Lily would, perhaps have done some things differently. She might have been able to save herself. But Lily, like so many women, would always be able to do for others what she could never do for herself.

Chapter 15
Fresno, California

Dr. Hale's office was soothingly tasteful — a low anxiety atmosphere. And Dr. Hale was soothingly tasteful himself in a murky gray three-piece suit and discreet bow tie. Every detail looked attended to except, surprisingly, his shoes, which were somewhat scabby-looking and scuffed. His diction was quite deliberate, his mouth moving to the extreme to accommodate the consonants.

"We have come to a point in Mizz — emphasizing the z's — O'Neil's treatment, where I think she could benefit from more direct contact with the community. She has progressed fairly well in the safe, structured environment of the hospital, and now she is ready, I believe, for some reality testing."

Dr. Hale stopped to peer over his glasses at Cassiopeia. "She would like very much to visit with your daughter, Mrs. Quinlan. Mizz O'Neil spoke extensively of Hope in treatment, and I believe, experienced some rather positive transference with the child prior to her breakdown."

Dr. Hale was quite disappointed to hear of

Hope's absence but encouraged a visit with Cassiopeia just the same. They arranged for Cassiopeia to come to the hospital during lunch the next day. Dr. Hale said that the best way to help Zona was to be encouraging and sincere.

"I might warn you Mrs. Quinlan, Mizz O'Neil may show some hostility. She is somewhat irrationally angry at the moment, and her confusion as to the cause of this anger may engender her misdirecting it at you. She is particularly impatient with anything she considers," — he paused and looked over the top of his glasses again — "what she calls 'bullshit.' "

The hospital, a sprawling, private facility on the outskirts of town, was stocked mostly by well-insured, upper-middle class to wealthy patients and resembled a small, rural college campus or, perhaps, a country club. It was staffed with attractive, officious-looking personnel with rubber-stamp smiles. Nursing staff did not wear uniforms and were recognizable only by the jangling keys clipped to their waists. A brisk, pretty nurse escorted Zona into the pastel foyer, where Cassiopeia waited.

"You must be Mrs. Quinlan." She didn't wait for a response but continued on, "She can't leave the grounds, but visit as long as you'd like. She's got until her two o'clock activity. See you then, Zona."

"Right," Zona said, her back to the nurse, her eyebrows lifted and eyes rolled upward. "Welcome to Camp Crazy, Cassie." Zona was smiling, but not completely in a good way. "Did you hear that? Visit as long as you like — until two o'clock. That's the kinda shit I can't stand here." She led Cassiopeia to a picnic table on a knoll, several hundred yards from the ward.

"It looks nice." Cassiopeia looked around them at the grassy slopes curving off to tennis and volleyball courts, low, slumpstone buildings, and a calm, sapphire pool.

"This is just the surface. Inside it's all rules, orders disguised as choices, and bullshit. They tell you everything is your choice, but God help you if you make the choice they don't like, which I always seem to do. I chose not to go to activities and got my status lowered fast. And God, Cassie you should see the activity people. Robots with degrees. They wanted me to do latch-hook, so I said 'I may be crazy, but I'm not stupid.' The leader didn't say a thing, just told my doc I was opposi-tional. They're all spies too." Zona, who had appeared almost too placid at first, now seemed to be working up to a lathered state of agitation. Her eyes snapped blue and flint-like. "This place sucks, Cassie. Everything I want to do is not . . ." She paused briefly and then spat the word. "Appropriate. And of course, they're all high priests of Appropriate."

"What about your doctor? He said you're making progress."

Zona broke into a wretched sort of laughter. "My insurance is running out, so I'm making progress. HA! Course sis'll pay for awhile. Our family's loaded you know."

"Yes, I met your sister. Gail. It's awfully nice of her to . . . '"

"Cassie, WAKE UP! Sometimes you're really naive. Gail wants me out of her hair, that's all. I could tell you stories about our family, Cassie. Set your ears on fire."

A papery white butterfly with black-tipped wings drifted by. Zona seemed to have lapsed into an angry silence.

Cassiopeia didn't know what to say. Finally, she said, "The doctor said you wanted to see Hope. I'm sorry she couldn't be here. I just put her on the plane to visit her godmother in Illinois. She'll be back soon," she lied. "It was so hot here, and her godmother called begging me to let her come visit."

Zona looked at Cassiopeia as if she hadn't heard any of this. "Look, I'm sorry I went off like that. I can't seem to learn to play the game like some people." The directness of her look was unsettling.

A tall woman, with short, brown hair shuffled up to them. She clutched a fake leopard coat tightly around herself, as if she thought it might come to life at any moment and try to escape. She might have been quite attractive once, but her face looked tired, visited too often by too many ghosts. She smiled foolishly, her eyes darting from side to side. "Nice tropical weather we're having."

"Hi, Faye," Zona said. "What's up?"

"That's a nice hat. Is that a sombrero?"

No one was wearing a hat, and Cassiopeia looked at Zona, who ignored this and repeated, "What's up, Faye?"

"Is it time for the two o'clock?" Faye asked, giggling out of the corner of her mouth.

When she left, Zona turned to Cassiopeia and smiled weakly. "I hope you're not sorry you came."

"No," said Cassiopeia. "I'd just like to see you

get well. I just wish it was better for you here."

"I don't fit in here, Cassie. Imagine that, to not fit in — in a mental hospital!" She laughed again, a low curdling gurgle. "You may be thinking, well who'd want to fit in anyway, but believe me, if you don't fit in here, you're in trouble."

"Does Faye fit in?"

"She fits in anywhere — or nowhere, which is better. She has her world inside. She wants nothing from them. All she needs is inside her. She's afraid they'll make her go, but she's got great insurance and a trust fund, too."

On the way home, Cassiopeia wondered, "Would I fit in there? Yes," she thought sadly. "I'd adapt, like I always do." She thought how sane and intelligent Zona sounded. She thought Zona had known somehow that she was lying to her. She felt bad and really wished that Hope could have come to see Zona. Somehow Hope had made a difference in Zona's life. Sometimes that happens, she thought, without anyone's being aware of it.

When Cassiopeia got home, the phone was ringing. "Mrs. Quinlan, I'm sorry I missed you at the hospital." It was Dr. Hale. "How was your visit with Mizz O'Neil?"

Was she being asked to report, to spy like Zona said? "It was fine, but I was surprised that she never mentioned Hope, and when I brought her up, she changed the subject."

"Uh huh . . ." Dr. Hale clicked his tongue into the receiver. "I'm not surprised. She was probably angry with you. That's her way of dealing with anger.

Complete avoidance. If something makes her angry, she immediately erases it from her memory and then, for her, it never happened. It's her way of taking control."

"But why would she be angry about my sending Hope to her godmother's?"

"Well, Mrs. Quinlan, like I said before, her anger is irrational and regressive, much like that of a three year old's. You were the instrument that interfered with the fulfillment of her desires. All that anger goes inside, though, and feeds her illness. It will most likely surface later in another form. But the head nurse reported that it was a successful visit, and she's maintained herself since returning to the ward."

"Dr. Hale, can you give me any idea how much longer she'll be at the hospital?"

A long pause. "I wish I could say. This has been a good week. If she continues this way, perhaps in a month or so — if she can achieve some treatment goals, that is."

Zona's right, Cassiopeia thought, hanging up. The world doesn't tolerate those who are different — not even a nut house. The last thing she'd said to Zona, was, "I admire you, Zona. This place isn't really going to change you. You'll be O.K. But I do know you've got to take your medication. Just cuz they're wrong about so much, doesn't mean they're wrong about that."

Zona's eyes filled, like melting pockets of ice. "Thanks Cassie, thanks for coming, for giving a shit."

It was time to get ready for work again. Marie had called that morning and asked if she could come in early. Cassiopeia laid out her black skirt and t-shirt with the orbiting satellite. She picked up the earrings. Cheap and silly, she thought, and flushed them down the toilet. Through the window, came the fumbled fingering of somebody practicing scales on a piano. For some reason Cassiopeia couldn't explain, the lonely notes falling like a broken string of pearls in the afternoon struck clear through to her soul. Her face was wet as she picked up the phone and dialed Juanita with panicky, trembling fingers. It rang for a frighteningly long time before Juanita answered. "

"Cassie, this is just plain uncanny. I've been trying to reach you all morning."

Cassiopeia interrupted. "Is everything all right? Is Hope . . ."

"Hope's fine. She's fine. She's right here helping me cook. We're fixing to take some food over to the Vale's. Cassie, something awful's happened."

Cassiopeia forgot her own panic attack, sensing something urgent in Juanita's voice. "It's Lily. She tried to kill herself last night. Her sister-in-law found her about one o'clock. Lily had called her earlier depressed about the sewer backing up, Eva said. Anyway, close to midnight, the phone rang again at Eva's, just once, woke her up though, and she had a bad feeling. She tried to call Lily's and got no answer, so she and Sam got dressed and drove over there. Oh, Cassie, it sounded awful. She . . . she . . ." Juanita was garbling her words and paused momentarily. Finally she went on. "She put a gun in her mouth and pulled the trigger. She's not dead. She's in a coma. Eva said one whole side of her face is practically gone."

Cassiopeia felt her stomach pitching and turning.

"Are you there, Cassie?"

Silence on both ends, then Juanita snuffled. "I'm still trying to find out more. Eva didn't seem to know much. If only I'd been home. Hope and I went into Chicago to visit my sister."

"Juanita, I'm sorry, really sorry. Is there anything I can do?" Casiopeia asked.

"Oh, I'll be O.K., girl. Cooking food to take to Eva's is keepin' me busy right now. She blames herself . . ." Juanita stopped.

"Now, don't *you* go blaming *yourself*," said Cassiopeia quickly. "Lily wouldn't want that."

"I'm working on it. But I think Hope has sensed something's not quite right. All morning she's been asking about that old yellow cat that's been gone now for a coupla weeks. I tried to explain a little bit of what's goin' on to her, but she don't say much and it's hard to know what all she's takin' in. Do you want to talk to her?"

Hope's voice sounded as small and distant as a baby cricket's, lost in the depth and immensity of timeless space. When Cassiopeia hung up the phone, she looked at the clothes on the bed waiting for her. She had called Juanita in a panic, fueled by a sort of delayed reaction to an accummulation of disappointments and a strange sense of water circling a drain, waiting to be sucked down by unseen forces.

Lily's suicide attempt scared her in a way she didn't fully comprehend. All these years she had carried a picture of Lily holding that gun in her hand and now it came to her again. Cassiopeia shivered despite the heat. She sat on the bed feeling dizzy and strange. She was worried, too. Juanita hadn't sounded too good. It was getting late. The last thing Cassiopeia felt like doing then was going to work, but she felt she owed it to Marie. Marie had fixed everything with Bud. Actually, he forgot the whole incident with Ned when, the very next week, his wife smashed up her Mercedes and landed in the hospital. This put a crimp in the whole divorce proceedings and turned Bud's attention elsewhere. The Satellite was slow, the rattle of liar's dice and chunks of ice in sweaty glasses one continuous loop linking all the usual bar sounds together in an overlap of sameness.

Driving home about one o'clock, Cassiopeia had the eerie sensation that she was watching herself from somewhere up above. Accelerate, slow, stop, turn. Tic, tic, tic. The streets seemed unfamiliar and strange. Tic. tic, tic. Palm, Olive, Linden. The neon globe of the Tower Theater hung moon-fuzzed and spellbound, clouded-over like a face vaguely familiar which one struggles to name. Cassiopeia continued slowly down Olive Street, not sure where she was going. She stopped at a red light and was gripped by a sudden, overwhelming nausea. Like lightning, it passed through her. The light hadn't changed and probably never would. Or it had changed, and she'd missed it.

There . . . foot to pedal. Careful now. She instructed the stranger at the wheel to pull over to the closest curb. "Who are you?" she screamed down at the slumped figure. "O.K., drive, whoever you are."

The figure obeyed and crept down Olive past the brightly deserted Mayfair Drugs. To her left, she saw a small bungalow and in the window outlined in neon *Palm Reader, Advisor, Horoscopes* in blue and red liquid lights that streamed into the darkness, and below this *Mrs. Katrina Raphael.*

"Stop here," she said, and the stranger did. "Get out of the car, go up the steps and knock on the door." The figure would not move. "Do it." She reached down to give the woman a push, but she was now out of the car, up the steps and across the stone porch pushing the buzzer. She watched herself on the porch, nervously backing away, and hissed, "You've come this far. Go on . . . Go on!"

Before she could escape, the door opened and an ordinary middle-aged woman with pink sponge curlers in her gray hair squinted out at her. "Mrs. Raphael is asleep," she said. "Can I help you?"

"I just wanted to ask her a few things," Cassiopeia heard herself saying.

"Well, you can ask me. I'm her assistant. Come in, come in . . ." She clucked Cassiopeia inside. She was short and pudgy and had on a wrinkled fuschia shift dress. She could have been anyone's grandma. The smell of used kitty litter permeated the room. "Sit, please," she waved to a rattan love seat in an alcove adjoining the front room. The furnishings were a mixture of faded floral forties and cheap Levitz modern with some sixties psychedelic accents. Mrs. Raphael's assistant adjusted her bifocals and peered at Cassiopeia like a diamond cutter assessing a gem.

"What is my name?" Cassiopeia asked suddenly, in a small, shaking voice. The assistant didn't hesitate.

"Your name comes from the sky. But I can tell

you this," she said in a hoarse whisper, "this is not your life. You're borrowing someone else's."

The vertigo was rising in Cassiopiea again. "What can I do?"

"You must find your true self," the assistant paused, leaning closer to Cassiopeia. "It's not here for you, my dear. There's been a terrible mistake. This happens. One lives under assumed names, identities. There are cases of double lives, secret lives, but that's not the case here. This is a clear case of . . ." she paused, rolled her fingertips together, then pressed them to her lips, ". . . a mistake. But it's not too late."

"So, what can I do?" Cassiopeia repeated.

Mrs. Raphael's assistant looked upset. "My dear, I'm very sorry. I should have explained. That's the future. That'll cost more money. The past is a special rate this week."

Cassiopiea thought that maybe she was joking, but there wasn't a trace of a smile on her lips. "How much do I owe so far?" She was getting nervous. She hadn't even thought to ask about money. "

"That'll be ten dollars. Do you want me to go on with the future?"

"I think I better stop there," Cassiopeia said, pulling some wrinkled bills and a handful of change out of her purse, money from her tips which she now counted out.

"I usually explain this right off, but I'm afraid I was still a bit groggy from being awakened. You really should make an appointment next time."

"I'm terribly sorry to have disturbed you." Cassiopeia was halfway to the door.

"Think nothing of it, my dear. Now, we're having a special on the future at the end of this month. You can come back then perhaps."

On the way home Cassiopeia noticed that both the vertigo and the voice from above were gone. At home, when she crawled into bed and closed her eyes, the fortune teller's assistant's words began to jumble together with the words of Juanita and Zona. "A terrible mistake, a terrible mistake" wove through it all in a jumbled refrain. Neither fully asleep nor entirely awake, Cassiopeia curled up in this babble as though she were the centrifugal center of an out-of-control carnival ride. In the morning, she woke with an unexpected sense of lightness and well-being. She hummed as she poured her coffee, rinsed off some plums, and opened the window to a citrus morning.

She thought of what Marie would say when she told her about the fortune teller's assistant charging her ten dollars to predict the past. A sudden image of Hap's wife pounding him with her cocktail purse appeared, and she almost choked on her coffee. Then she found herself laughing so hard her stomach muscles cramped. She watched the neighbor's cat, the one Zona called The Terminator, stalk a mockingbird. The bird just squawked and flashed away. Cassiopeia heard the piano scales meandering in again. Some child in the neighborhood, sitting in a spillway of sun and dust practicing for a lesson.

Her thoughts drifted to Lily. Juanita had said that Lily could be in the coma indefinitely. "How awful," she thought, "to be lying there, unaware of the sun through hospital windows, the peppermint antiseptic coolness, the squish, squish of the nurse's steps, dependent as a tube-fed preemie. Far better to feel the pain."

Before Cassiopeia left her, Zona told her that she was not to worry. "I'll pull it off, you'll see. I want my own place back. I liked having things to worry about, take care of. At least there I could control the weeds, the ants, the thermostat, answer the phone only if it pleased me. It was a small empire, but I was the Empress."

Cassiopeia thought of Mrs. Raphael's assistant, of Juanita's strained voice, and Hope's minute one. It was like a series of little sounds going off in her head. Click, click, click, click, click. She thought of the word she'd run across in an astronomy book the other day and had to look up: synergism - The action of two or more substances, organs, or organisms to achieve an effect of which each is individually incapable. She picked up the telephone. "A few phone calls," she thought. "All I have to do is dial the right numbers."

Chapter 16

•

Bakersfield, California

Wally's passion, perhaps his only one, was fishing. Eileen had taken it up at first just to be with him and had been surprised to find that she enjoyed herself waiting for a catfish to strike, watching the dull canal's face pocked with muddy clouds. Wally and Eileen both worked nights, Wally as a night watchman, and Eileen as a nurse's aide. In the daytime, they either slept or fished, or both.

Cassiopeia had come to live with them after spending a summer and a miserable freshman year of high school in Chevyville with Juanita while Eileen took off for Bakersfield with Wally. She'd met him in Moline, but he had already made plans to move back to his hometown, where they married and took up their simple life of work and fishing.

Cassiopeia was suffering from a sense of not fitting in anywhere, due partly to adolescence and partly to their previous gypsy life. Eileen had shuttled her back and forth between California, Illinois, and Mississippi all her life, and now she was not sure where she belonged. And she was afraid to settle herself into life at the Rainbow Trailer Court with Eileen and Wally for fear that as soon as she did, Eileen would be on to something or somewhere else.

When Cassiopeia got home from school, she had to tiptoe around the trailer, watching American Bandstand with the sound turned down. Eileen and Wally's snores seeped under the flimsy bedroom door. It was their habit to take off fishing when they each got off work in the morning and then come home to nap. On their days off together, they left before dusk, setting up aluminum chairs on the canal bank, lighting gas lanterns, and tossing in their lines. They asked Cassiopeia to come, but she refused, half wanting to go but feeling too old to tag along.

One evening after they'd gone, Cassiopeia rearranged her room, flipped through *Seventeen*, polished her nails, and wrote a report on the circulatory system for her health class. When she'd finished, she stepped outside into the fiery dusk and sat on the trailer's aluminum steps. "Who can I count on if I can't count on you? I never counted on you makin' me blue," Patsy Cline twanged out from someone else's trailer. Three grimy little boys scooted by in a rusted wagon tied to the bumper of a Volkswagon driven by a crew-cut boy who couldn't possibly have had his license.

Cassiopeia had been at the Rainbow Trailer Court almost a month, and so far she'd seen only families with little kids or older adults. She felt as if she were convalescing: lots of bed rest, boring food, as little excitement as possible. If only a talent scout would spot her and put her in the movies, or if only a cute boy would walk by. The phone was ringing. She raced inside, banging aluminum against aluminum. It was Lupe.

"Hi, what're you doing?"

"Nothing. What are you doing?"

"Nothing. Why don't you come over?"

"I can't. My parents aren't home."

"They're always gone," Lupe said. "Hey, you can get back before they come home. They'll never know."

Cassiopeia hung up and sat on her narrow, pom-pom pink bed. They all lived in their own separate worlds even though occupying the same cramped trailer space. Being ignored had its advantages, but somewhere behind lurked the misunderstood ghost of resentment who whispered in her ear, "They really just don't care. Why don't you show them."

"Why not?" she thought, and began packing her plaid, zippered suitcase with pajamas, school clothes, toothbrush and school books. She pried the rubber stopper off her Elvis bank and stuffed bills and coins into a sock at the bottom of her bag. Forty some minutes later, she was on Lupe's front porch with her bag. When Lupe came to the door, grinning conspiratorially, Cassiopeia said, "I've run away from home. Can I stay here?"

"Sure," said Lupe without hesitation. "We'll just tell Mom you're spending the night while your folks are out of town." Mrs. Olivera was short and round and dyed her hair a different color every week. This week the brown had been frosted with silver.

"You like it?" she asked Cassie. "Cost me thirty bucks, but I'm worth it, I say to myself. They put this leetle hat on me with holes punched in it all over, pulled my hair out the holes. I looked like Boo Boo the clown."

"Bozo, Mom," Lupe corrected impatiently. The best thing about Mrs. O. was that she asked very few questions, accepting all their scams at face value, allowing them to get away with murder while she ate chocolate doughnuts and watched "The Beeg Valley." She stocked the cupboards with cookies, sodas, Twinkies, and Cheeze Puffs. The house was a spacious — three bedrooms, two baths — but dilapidated tract home with one toilet that didn't flush and a swimming pool, usually scummed on the bottom with algae. Cassiopeia and Lupe had swum in it only once. "Just don't touch bottom," Lupe said.

Mrs. O., her feet propped up on pillows, sat on the crushed velvet sofa below a portrait in which she was swallowed in a huge, white, fake fur coat with Lupe and her two little brothers gathered like cubs around a polar bear. Mr. O., known in the family as "the infidel," had deserted them after the second boy was born.

Cassiopeia put her bag in Lupe's blue and magical room. Lupe had draped flowing scarves over the doorways and billowed the ceiling with yards of a frothy blue material Mrs. O. had rescued from a fabric store fire sale. Here and there, faint, scorched clouds undulated in the breeze coming in the windows. Lupe had a row of Virgin Marys lined up like white, veiled brides on her windowsill. Reigning over this harem like an Arabian rock and roll fantasy was a large, glossy portrait of Elvis.

"Ma, we're gonna cook. We're hungry," Lupe called from the kitchen.

"There's all kinds of stuff to eat. I don't want you cooking, Lupe. You make a mess." But she never budged from the sofa, and Lupe went on, pulling down pudding mix, chocolate chips, marshmallows, and canned frosting. Lupe made the pudding with ice cream instead of milk. Cassiopeia melted the marshmallows and chocolate chips together, and they layered it all in a loaf pan, stuck it in the freezer for fifteen minutes, and then rolled out dollops of whipped cream all over the top. Lupe stacked pans, bowls, and sticky spoons in the sink. Chocolate and marshmallow dribbled over the counters and down the side of the fridge. They carried the loaf pan and two spoons into her room and shut the door then lay on Lupe's bed eating right from the pan while Lupe talked about boys and Cassiopeia listened.

Eileen didn't really like Lupe much, saying she was "boy crazy" and accusing her of being behind every new teen-age habit Cassiopeia aquired, from wearing make-up to talking on the phone. Every time the phone rang, Lupe dived for it in case it was Eileen. They had agreed Lupe would lie and say that Cassiopeia wasn't there, and she hadn't seen her. Cassiopeia had left no note. She just shut her bedroom door and left.

In the morning, she and Lupe made their own breakfast — lemon yogurt, frosted flakes and chocolate sprinkles — and went off to school. Mrs. O. had already gotten the boys off and left for her job as secretary at an insurance company. That night, Lupe begged, singing, "We want the Colonel. We want the Colonel," until Mrs. O. went out and bought a giant bucket of Kentucky Fried Chicken with rolls, mashed potatoes, and gravy. After dinner they watched t.v., although Mrs. O. told them, shortly before she fell asleep on the gold carpet while watching *The Newlywed Game*, that they had to get their homework done first.

"She'll call tonight for sure," Cassiopeia said. "You have to sound convincing, Lupe. If she finds out, I'll be grounded for the rest of my life." Of course they ignored the fact that sooner or later Eileen would find out, unless, of course, Cassiopeia never went back, and this never entered her head. But by twelve o'clock they were all asleep on the living room floor, even Lupe's little brothers, and the phone hadn't rung even once.

When Lupe and Cassiopeia got home from school the next day, they put a stack of Elvis records on the stereo. "Let's try on clothes," Lupe said. "Here, try on this skirt and this sweater, Cassie. You'd look cute in that lilac." They didn't hear Lupe's little brothers come home from school an hour later, or the ringing of the telephone, and when Timmy stuck his head in the door and said "Phone for Cassie" they both just froze.

"I could say Timmy made a mistake." Lupe offered.

"No, I better go." Cassiopeia didn't know what to expect. Eileen's usual punishment was to put her to work, but she'd never pulled anything like this before. When she came back into the bedroom, Lupe looked scared.

"What'd she say?"

Cassiopeia started packing. "She just said I better get home right away."

"If you want, you can borrow that outfit," Lupe said.

When Cassiopeia arrived at the trailer, she could hear Wally snoring in the bedroom, but there was no sign of Eileen. Cassiopeia unpacked and sat on her bed waiting. Finally, at least a half hour later, she heard noises in the kitchen and waited again until Eileen was at her door. Cassiopeia tried to compose her face to look remorseful.

"What's wrong with you? You look like you've been up to something," Eileen said. "Where'd you get those clothes?"

"They're Lupe's," Cassiopeia said.

"Well, you can just give them right back. I don't like you borrowing clothes. And you better call next time you go to Lupe's after school." Eileen was gone again. Stunned into silence, Cassiopeia listened to her banging cupboards, unloading groceries in the kitchen.

Was it possible? Yes. They could have come home from work, gone fishing while she was in school, come back home and gone to bed, gotten up and gone to work again assuming she was in her room asleep.

Eileen was calling her. It was one of Cassiopeia's jobs to help unload groceries. "Here, you finish up. I'm beat." Eileen half laid on the sofa across from the kitchen, which was all really one room. "Wally and I are both off tomorrow night, Cassie. Wanna come fishing with us? We're going over to Delta Mendota. Friend of Wally's says they've been pulling ten pound cats outta there lately. Why don't you come with us?"

Cassiopeia stole a glance at Eileen. There was no sign she knew. "O.K." she said, with a guilty kind of relief. She still didn't really want to go, but felt a weak superstition that the gods who had given her this reprieve would want her to say yes. Later that night, after Wally had gone to work, Eileen smoked a cigarette outside on the porch, and Cassiopeia ran to the phone and called Lupe. "I'm grounded for the weekend," she said.

"That's all? Wow, are you lucky. My mom'd kill me." So they both lied, Lupe, knowing her own mother would be easily fooled and Cassiopeia too embarrassed to tell Lupe that her mother had never missed her. Cassiopeia never told Eileen that she had run away from home, but she always felt secretly cheated and never quite forgave her for it.

The next day was an ordinary Saturday. Cassiopeia helped Eileen clean house. Around three o'clock, they got their gear together and headed out, bouncing over back roads in Wally's pickup, Wally saying almost nothing except to once ask Eileen if she wanted the window rolled up more. Cassiopeia couldn't understand why they had to drive so far. There were plenty of canals they could go to nearer to home. Alkaline dust drifted into the cab, flouring them with a fine, gray talc. They drove straight into the sun bouncing on the horizon, its great bubble leaking a red-orange tinge into the sky. As it sunk lower, the sky went all crazy in a riot of purples and reds, as if the sun had burst, spraying out its colors. Cassiopeia sank down lower herself, and gradually Eileen stopped trying to chatter about nothing. They finally came to a halt, showered in dust and silence.

A string of campers and pick-ups dotted the canal bank already. They set up their woven chairs, Wally sucking his false teeth while music from a Spanish radio station beat nearby. A brood of dark-skinned children scratched in the dust, shrieked in Spanish, and chased one another down the canal. Cassiopeia felt bored and out of place. Everyone here was either foreign or old, it seemed to her. Wally baited her line with a fat, pink nightcrawler, boring the hook into its middle, the ends flopping. The sky still clung to its light, even as night made its presence known. Eileen was instructing Cassiopeia in the art of cat fishing, as if she knew it all, to Cassiopeia's repeated, "I'm not a retard, Mom."

A low, worried buzz came nearer and nearer, filling the sky and they looked up to see a crop duster dancing under a wire, then zipping straight down the canal strafing them like a berserk mosquito. Dust flew as everyone ran and dived for cover. Cassiopeia threw herself on their ratty, old bedspread and covered her head. Eileen screamed and screamed. Up it went again, circling, then zooming back down the canal, in a low, whining drone that left a dust devil wind and a cloud of fumes. Again and again it buzzed them, darting off as suddenly as it had struck.

"What the hell . . ." was all Eileen could say, looking to Wally for answers. Cassiopeia stayed down on the blanket, her pole thrown down.

"Some fool crop duster. Probably been drinking again," was all Wally said.

"It's a wonder we weren't all killed. That's dangerous. Who does he think he is . . ." Eileen went on for some time in this vein.

Wally retrieved Cassiopeia's pole, and set her up again, the dark now dropped fully around them. Gas lanterns twinkled on up and down the bank and serious cat fishing resumed. After awhile, Cassiopeia felt the flow of the water lulling her, the line singing through her fingers. Each time she thought she felt a tugging on her line, she reeled it in to stolen bait or a handful of snagged weeds.

"It's like a sharp tap, when they hit," Wally told her. "And then your pole tip'll bend way over. Give it a good, quick jerk to set the hook, then let out a little line. Ole mama catfish'll think she's gettin away then and swallow the hook. And then you got 'er. Just sit back and reeeel it on in." Wally winked at Cassiopeia like they had a secret between them.

It was the first time he'd spoken more than half a dozen words to her. Cassiopeia did not dislike Wally and really had no feelings for or against him at all. Wally, for his part, was terrified of anyone who didn't fish. But, that night they had all faced death together, no matter if Eileen had proved less than a good soldier. They had all fished together, and on the way back Wally drove through the sweetest night he'd ever known, the girls asleep beside him, a big, yellow moon pulsing through alfalfa winds, and a string of catfish trailing them all the way home.

Chapter 17
Chevyville, Illinois

The day had begun strangely gray and benign for August. Mornings were Lily's favorites, but this one had no early singing light, as if all creation were a liturgical choir. Lily Vale had escaped from the mire of a swampy dream. All night, a muttering wind sucked at the hem of her gown, causing her to roll into awkward positions. Seeking solace and warmth, she had wrapped herself in her own arms, and woke that way, with her neck stiff and cricked.

She had spent the past week wading through a lifetime of accumulations, boxing up cross-stitched linens, sway-back books, overcoats, fat-heeled boots, baby booties, old Mason jars gummy-thick with dust, kitchen utensils, tools of mysterious origin and function, a set of blue canary Noritake dishes, and an unfinished bedspread with the crochet hook still caught in a chain. She had even found a set of false teeth of unknown ownership in a drawer.

This was the house she had brought her new babies to, all four carried up the wide, concrete slab steps of the porch while Lester put the car away. Lester had his routines, and nothing, not natural disasters, national emergencies, or new babies disrupted them. With Ephrim, the last, Lily had felt the porch slipping away while she fumbled with the house key. Lester found her crumpled against the door, Ephrim clamped safely in the vise of her enclosing arms.

And she remembered the porch again, three months later, swaying off kilter like a tipped deck when they had taken Ephrim away to be launched into the darkness where she could not keep him safe from the cold bite of wind and ice. Crib death, they said. No cause. No explanation. As if the crib, with its line-dried sheets where she tucked him so trustingly, were at fault. Her breasts were left aching with fullness, her arms aching with emptiness.

Ephrim had been a late-in-life baby. The youngest of the other three was eighteen and the oldest twenty-seven. Lily was forty-four and despite some of her women friends' disapproval, she had been thrilled with the prospect of another child.

This one could be different. She would pawn her soul to make it so. The others had never been hers. Lester's mother, Ida, had come to help with Tony and stayed off and on through two more births until her own death six months before Ephrim was born. In fact, when the news of Ida's death was broken to her, almost Lily's first thought had been that this child could be all hers now. She always thought that if Ida had known of her pregnancy, she'd have figured out a way not to go so soon.

Lester lost his hold over her, too, after Ida's death. Lily no longer cared if he drank himself blind. He wasn't abusive like he had been when the children were younger, and somehow he kept working at the plant, using his free time to get drunk. But after his mother's death and Lily's announcement of the pregnancy, Lester tried to put away the bottles he had managed for so long to stack between himself and Ida and Lily — a wall of liquid and glass.

And when he discovered Lily no longer cared enough to bother hiding his booze, in fact would probably just as soon buy it for him herself, it was all the more reason to quit. When the last bottle was emptied, he bought no more and for the next six months, he repaired plumbing that had leaked for years, replaced shingles and broken window glass. He saw his surroundings for the first time, without the obliterating veil of alcohol.

And he tried to make amends with Lily, but she ignored him, lost in obsessive preparations for the baby. Lester could not remember a night with Lily that would have produced this pregnancy but couldn't admit this and joined perplexedly in the buying, borrowing, and fixing up. Lily, sensing her new power, reigned with superiority laced with a touch of contempt. She moved into Tony's old room with only a bed and a dresser and wouldn't let Lester near her at night for fear of losing the child. Lily sewed new curtains and quilted a spread, painted walls and hung bright mobiles for the nursery. A friend of Juanita's cut Mother Goose characters from wood. Lily painted them and hung them on the wall. Juanita gave her a baby shower, cracking jokes about Lily's being a new mother when she should be becoming a grandmother.

Juanita and Lily had become friends a few years before after years of being enemies when Lily's car had broken down not far from Juanita's. Juanita had stopped to help, not even knowing it was Lily. They were both slightly embarrassed, but Juanita had taken her home to call a tow truck, and while they waited, Juanita talked Lily into a hot toddy. It was a cold, wet-to-the-bone October night, and after the tow truck came and took the car away, Lily had stayed on by the crackling fire surprised at the ease and veracity of their conversation.

Suddenly Juanita said, "How come you always hated me in school, Lily?"

"I didn't. You hated me," Lily said, surprised at Juanita's candidness.

Juanita had on her silky, Cheshire cat grin. "Guess I didn't trust anybody who was Mary Beth's friend."

"Mary Beth's a stinking, two-faced weasel." It was hard to surprise Juanita, but she just sat there with her mouth open. "I guess I should explain," said Lily then. She told how she had made the wedding dresses for all Mary Beth's girls until Mary Jo, second to the youngest got engaged. "I didn't mind, really. I never asked for money. It was such fun helping pick out the pattern, the fabric and hearing all their bridal chit-chat while I pinned up the hems, tucked and basted. Then, watching the dress take shape, I loved getting it just right, and sometimes they'd ask my advice 'bout this or that. Course on the big day, knowing my creation was the center of it all, flash bulbs and champagne popping. And the compliments. I liked it all right. It was like it was happening to me but without the bad ending."

Juanita was listening, completely attentive and silent. "Well, anyway, with Mary Jo, it was different. She picked some fancy designer pattern and made all these changes to boot. Lengthen the waistline a bit, scallop this, shorten that, add different sleeves, change the neckline. I got a kind of feel for how it'd look, and she didn't at all, but she wouldn't listen to nothin' I said. Nearly put my eyes out juggling pattern pieces together, gettin' her in to try it on at each step cause I was really making the whole darn pattern over. And she acted real put out, too, like she was doin' me a favor. Well, to get on, I got it all done and it fit her to a T. Turned out real nice, after all that fussing, too, and five weeks later, Mary Beth calls up and says cool as can be can I make some adjustments. But it fit perfect, I say. So then Mary Beth kind of laughs and says well not anymore. Mary Jo's pregnant. Can't get it zipped up. This is three weeks before the ceremony. Well, I didn't care about her bein' pregnant, but shoot . . . all that work. There was nothin' else to do though. I set about with the pins and seam ripper. God, what a job. Way worse than makin' it in the first place, and that was no picnic. And I wasn't real happy with it. That delicate fabric didn't take well to being messed with so much. I did the best I could though. Let out every seam possible. Mary Jo was lookin' like she'd been eating for triplets, too, nice and thick round the middle. I worked on it though, day and night, even managed to work in some pleats to help disguise the condition."

"I hope Mary Beth appreciated all that," Juanita said suspiciously.

"She was tickled with the way it looked, but I don't think she realized how much trouble it was. Well, week and a half after that, about three days before the wedding, I got up one morning, sick as a dog. I had that stomach flu going around. Then Ida got down in her back. She was with us at the time, and she always expected me to wait on her when that happened. Well, 'bout noon, Mary Beth called. I barely made it to the phone, and she starts off laughing. 'Guess what?' she says, 'Mary Jo miscarried three days ago. She hasn't eaten for over a week and lost a good ten pounds, so the dress just swims on her now.' Then she says, 'Looks like it's back to the cutting board, Lily.' Says Mary Jo's on her way over with the dress. All the time laughing like it was the best joke. When I finally got a chance, I just told her I couldn't do it, I was sick. 'But what'll we do?' she says in that high voice a hers. I just said, 'I don't know, Mary Beth. I've got to hang up though 'cuz I'm fixing to throw up all over the phone.' Mary Jo shows up while I'm in the bathroom, and when I tell her, she just says, real huffy-like, 'Wish I'd a known before I drove all the way over here.' Says she'll ask Lorna Chenowith. Maybe she won't let her down. And she whips out the door and out of the driveway like hell on wheels. And do you know, day before the cermeony, Mary Beth calls me to say I'm being uninvited to the wedding cuz Mary Jo wouldn't feel comfortable with me there. Makes like it's all Mary Jo but makes sure to tell me they had to go into the city and pay double to find someone to alter the dress on such short notice."

"That's awful, Lily. She's gotten worse, if that's possible."

"Well, you know, I got to thinking back after that and decided Mary Beth never really was my friend, not less she needed something. And get this . . . now SHE won't speak to ME!"

They talked on then, reminiscing about people they both knew, and found themselves crying, as much for the loss of their green and distant days as anything. Juanita brought up Russell Haycraft's funeral and the sting of bitter tears washed mid-stream into laughter.

"I still have a bald spot in back there where you yanked out my hair," Lily said.

"I did you a favor," Juanita laughed, "You've got enough hair for all the bald men in Texas, Lily."

After Lily left that night, Juanita sat a long time watching the waning embers in the fireplace. She had really not hated Lily all those years. They had just avoided each other, as much out of habit as anything else.

They became friends after that, as if all those years had never intervened. When Ephrim died, Juanita was the only one who seemed to understand the impact of that loss on Lily.

"She was too old to bring up a child, anyway," the pastor's wife had the misfortune to say in front of Juanita.

"Mothering knows no age, but tolerance does. And I believe I'm gettin' too old to put up with you," Juanita snapped.

There was a new emptiness to the house after Ephrim died. It was empty in a way it had never been with the other children's leaving. Lily had never made anything happen for herself, always waiting to fit into

Ida's or Lester's plans, always doing for someone else. Ephrim was to be her new life, and when he was gone the future collapsed. Lester went back to the bottle on a marathon drunk, non-stop for two solid weeks, and landed in the veteran's hospital de-tox unit after Lily found him face down halfway into the baby crib and an inch away from death.

Lester had been in his new place, a rehab referral house, for about three months. "He might be there for years," Dr. Swann said when Lily met with him. He said Lester needed extensive treatment. Insurance would not cover all of it, and he recommended selling the house as "the best solution for everyone." It made perfect, logical sense. The children were scattered all over. They almost never came home or even called. And maybe she could exorcize some ghosts, Lily thought to herself.

When Lester was ushered into the office by a stern-looking nurse, Lily looked at him with his smart, new haircut and wearing an Old Spice-drenched shirt she had never seen before, making eye contact only with the onyx clock on Dr. Swann's grass-cloth wall. "I have come to know my oldest enemy," she thought, "and he is the man I've lived with for over twenty years but who I'll never know."

A vague memory of the dream kept sneaking up on her all morning, a murkiness with layers of maliferous fog waiting behind the surface, a window with a reptilian eye and her dead mother's faint voice in the background calling for help from far away. A swampy heaviness pulled at and incapacitated her. Like a dull headache, it surfaced off and on, just enough to interfere as she moved about packing and labeling boxes. A groggy tiredness weighed her down, and her neck was filled with a constant searing pain. All morning, she felt a curious sensation of inner motion, too, a motion to which the pulse in her temples seemed to be keeping time. While carrying Ephrim, she'd suffered a mild stroke. The doctor had discovered it during one of her check-ups, toward the end of her pregnancy and ordered her to bed. Juanita had come in to help every day, but Lily had told no one of the stroke. It was her worst fear, being old and dependent.

At noon, she stopped to fix herself lunch, but the bread of her sandwich seemed to be expanding in her mouth as she chewed, and she threw it away. Food often lacked appeal for her these days. She couldn't seem to shake a nagging, unspecific fear that swam in her stomach like a spawning fish. On her way to the garage about two o'clock, her foot came up wet and muddy as she walked across the lawn. Stooping down, she saw that she was at the edge of an oily pool of sludge about three feet across. She took a stick and poked, stirring up nothing, but mush and what looked like excrement.

"Oh God, it's the sewer backing up," she thought disgustedly. As she stood, silver spots danced in the air and the ground reached up for her. It was only a second or two that she was out, but her stomach was really thrashing as she made her way to the house. Inside, Lily laid on the sofa, trying to catch her breath. She thought of calling Juanita but remembered that she had taken Hope in to visit her sister in Chicago for a few days and wouldn't be back till the next morning. She finally called Eva, Lester's sister, but told her only about the sewer. Nothing in Eva's voice encouraged her to say more.

When Lily hung up the phone, she thought, "I've got to pull myself together. This is silly. The sewer's backed up. So what? And I'm probably just over-doing. I'll try and take a nap." She was awakened by Lorna Chenowith calling to cancel their dinner that night because she had too much to do. Lily was annoyed. Here she was packing up to move over twenty years of her life, and she'd been willing to take out a couple of hours for dinner. At least, she thought, Lorna could have made up a decent excuse. She was still gnawing this aggravation bone when Lester called.

Since his new recovery, he'd taken to calling her up daily, usually about some mundane detail to do with the house or car. She hated these calls. Lester had grown increasingly rigid and petty as he progressed in treatment, even though, or perhaps because, he had given up the alcohol. Some days he was full of contrition and self-condemnation, calling himself worse names than she'd ever thought of. Lily just wished he'd leave her alone. She wanted only to live in peace and quiet now.

"I was thinkin'," he said, "'bout Ephrim's things. What're you gonna do with 'em?"

A long sigh ushered forth from Lily. Today she did not want to even think about it. "Juanita said she'd help me figure it out when the time came."

"Well, I had a session 'bout Ephrim."

"Oh no," she thought.

"And I think we should burn all that stuff, just

get rid of it, make a . . ."

Lily cut in. "No. That may be what you think would be good for you, but I don't want it burned."

Lester was silent. Lily was not usually that definite. "You know, it may be diseased," he started on a new tack.

"I don't want to discuss this, Lester."

"We can't put it off forever. I'll get someone to do it for us. You won't have to do a thing. What difference does it make anyway?"

She felt the pain in her neck pivoting in like a predator, seeking the weakest point, the fish turning over in her stomach. "I won't argue," she thought. And finally, Lester broke the volatile silence.

"Just think it over, O.K.?"

He hadn't given up yet. "Good bye, Lester," she said with a firm click. Then to herself out loud, "I won't have it. I just won't."

She found herself heading for Ephrim's room. She hadn't been in there for over four months, not since the morning she'd found him, pale and uncrying, in the crib. The full flush of that horror came back as she stood under the twinkling baby lambs and chicks. There was the plywood cow straddling the crescent moon, the lamp with cut-outs of stars where the light spilled through, the dresser she'd painted herself still lined with stacks of diapers and receiving gowns. She dragged in boxes and ruthlessly began to pack. She did not cry. She lugged each box down the stairs herself and loaded them into the trunk of the car, and drove to Juanita's. Calmer now, she even hummed along with the radio. At Juanita's she stacked the boxes on her porch and taped a note to the top.

When she finally got back to the house, it was totally dark, with a web of brilliant stars overhead. She looked up and saw the Milky Way like the lonely blaze of a distant city. It was late and she'd hardly eaten all day, but Lily didn't feel hunger. She sat on the sofa in the dim living room, shadows and occasional lights from the street bathing her as they washed over the walls. The muscles in her neck shuddered. Her entire body was a tight fist, and yet she felt strangely calm and detached, almost happy.

Lester's hip boots leaned casually against the wall with boxes of old, cobwebby tackle. She had packed his things and stacked them there together. There was surprisingly little: some graying underwear; bleached overalls; some morosely dark, wide, satin ties; a box of unopened gift colognes; a box of coins; cracked spectacles; and old war medals, one of which said "For Courage Under Difficult Circumstances." His service revolver was there where she had kept it, hidden in a box of tissue paper all these years, with a box of shells.

"There are many reasons to do it," she thought. "That's no problem."

Since Ephrim's death, these thoughts had been her only refuge at times. Many hours she had consoled herself by planning how. She decided a gun was the surest way. She thought of it as escape, not suicide. When she walked alone at dusk, watching the neighborhood blinking on like warm cells against the hive of night, she planned her escape with serenity and relief. Now she was grasping for a reason not to escape. But so much pain had flooded in on her in one day, with no relief in sight. She picked up the phone, dialed Eva's number, then hastily hung up.

If only Juanita were home. Several times after a walk, she had called Juanita, and Juanita, sensing something, had cracked a joke and laughed or just said, "I'm coming over."

It had been Juanita's child-laugh that had defused things for her. Somehow, the ordinariness of the world then defied human tampering. Once she'd remarked casually to Juanita that sometimes she didn't feel like going on, and Juanita just said, "Stick around, kid. The second feature is always better."

But Lily had a deep suspicion that the second feature was not to be in this life, and now as she sat in the dark living room, stray car lights criss-crossing the walls, she thought how much the room resembled a darkened movie theater. A compelling curiosity mingled with a nervous kind of excitement and peace. "I need a sign," she thought finally, and flicked the remote button. Maybe a sign would come to her from the t.v.

At her command, the darkened corner filled with brilliant colors and artificial laughter. A comedian wordlessly moved his lips. Click. The weather man was posed before a colorful map of the U.S., computer simulated clouds and high pressure zones predicting no real change for the week-end. Click. "Get ready for the coming of Jesus . . ." An eight hundred number and send your contribution. Click. ". . . can quickly and easily pull those highlights out, load the palette knife," (zoom into a globby copse of sap green and umber). Click ". . . genuine freshwater pearls, six strands, store owners must be shocked at our price. . . Thank you for calling Home Shopping Club . . . first time you wore it, it broke . . . nothing in life is perfect. Just mail it back to us. Now folks, I'm going to cut prices like crazy." A slender, disembodied hand slithered up the velvet, headless bust and fondled the freshwater pearls. Click. A cuddly, cute baby popped out of a tire, toddled over and reached toward the screen. Click. The dazzling, snowy buzz of nothingness. Click.

Juanita sat beside Lily at the hospital, holding her unresponsive hand. "Was Lily a coward, or indeed, very brave? I just don't know," thought Juanita. "I prefer to think she was very brave, that anaemic school girl with the timid blue eyes." Juanita's face was filled with tears, Lily's wrapped in a halo of gauze, her head shaved, her eyes unblinking, staring up into orderly rows of flourescense. Juanita had seen a look like that once on a man's face. He had just come out of her and having extricated himself, was anxious to return to the world that he owned and controlled. He lay in the tall Johnson grass, eyes fixed like a broken compass, staring straight up. Teasing, she had thrown his t-shirt over her eyes. "Where are you? I can't see you. Everything's gone dark," she said.

"I'm right here," he replied.

"No you're not, you're a million miles away," she said sadly, pulling the t-shirt off.

"You're a witch," he said, "and I'm undoing your spell."

"Where are you, Lily, where are you? I can't see you. It's dark . . ."

Chapter 18

•

Fresno, California

Cassiopeia had gotten the letter when she was in the midst of preparations to leave. The handwriting was scary: big, loopy, out of the past. Cassiopeia took the letter from the mailman and opened it right on the porch. It was from Wally's sister in Bakersfield, writing for Wally, who was in a Fresno rest home . . . not doing well . . . and he wanted to see her. There wasn't much time left. She went directly inside and changed out of her sweaty work clothes and took a bus across town since she'd already sold her car. Cassiopeia had not seen or heard from Wally since before she left Bakersfield. After Hope was born, she'd taken her to see him a few times, but he had never really recovered from a series of operations shortly after Eileen's death.

At the rest home, Cassiopeia talked to a very young nurse, who thanked her for coming. Leading Cassiopeia down a long hall, she said, "He's one of my favorite patients. Not a talker, that's for sure, but such a pleasant man. His sister's been coming when she can, but she's not in the best of health either. Frankly," the nurse stopped and turned to look directly at Cassiopeia, "we don't expect him to last much longer."

Wally's room contained nothing of him but his being, and even that had changed. He'd aged so much in the last few years that Cassiopeia would hardly have recognized him, and there were new signs of pain etched into his already deeply grooved face. His smile when he saw her was quiet but large, if somewhat unfocused.

"Good to see you Cassie . . . so good. Thanks for coming."

"I didn't even know you were here, or I'd have come sooner. How did your sister get my address?"

"She's a pretty sharp cookie." He paused, "She wrote to Juanita." It took a minute for Cassiopeia to see that it was a joke. Then she laughed, and he seemed very pleased.

An old lady was moaning, just outside the door, in the hall. "Help me, oh, help me someone . . . I've soiled myself . . . please, please help me." The moaning turned into a low, gurgling whimper.

"Mrs. Trumble," Wally said. "She's kind of nuts. Always thinks she's soiled herself, but far as I know, she never does. The nurses are very good to us here. I'm real lucky. It's no Madonna Inn," he said as he pointed to the chipped, water-stained ceiling, "but lotsa nice folks here."

"Funny, they say the same about you."

Wally blushed. "Say, did you know we was at the Madonna Inn for our honeymoon? What a place that is. Eileen loved it. We danced in that big ole ballroom after dinner with all the twinkly lights, just like

Christmas. Eileen ordered a champagne cocktail. I'll
never forget, cuz I ordered me a beer, and she had the
biggest fit you ever saw. That was my girl, hankering
after steak and champagne when all I wanted was beer
and a hot dog." Wally chuckled. "She was quite a girl
though."

Wally's eyes had grown cloudy as clabbered
milk, and Cassiopeia wondered if the fuzziness didn't
extend beyond just failing eyesight. His picture of
Eileen was quite different from hers. "What a temper
she had. All show you know."

"No," Cassiopeia thought, "I didn't know."

"Sure wish she could a seen little Hope. She'd a
gone nuts over her. How's she doing?"

Cassiopeia pulled out some pictures, wondering, would she, would she have gone nuts over her?
"I'm sorry Hope couldn't come with me, but she's gone
back to visit Juanita for awhile."

Wally held the pictures up close to his milky
eyes. "Ain't she somethin'. Favors Eileen, you know."

"Not really. At least I don't see it," she thought
to herself. "You can keep that one. It's the latest. I've
got more." Wally propped it up against a bottle of pills
on the nightstand. "How are you feeling, Wally?" She
had never been able to call him Dad, and it felt too
strange to start now.

"Oh, up and down. I"m better today. They keep
plugging me with pills. Ever day I tell 'em this time I got
me a ache you ain't got no pill fer, but they always do."
He waved to the table and an array of bottles and vials.
"All colors, you name it . . . heart, liver, kidneys, thyroid,
digestion, blood pressure . . . you take my pills away, I

betcha I'd shut down faster than a henhouse without a rooster." The flood of speech halted as Wally stared someplace between his glazed over eyes and the filmy hospital curtains. "They was a ring . . ." an effort had crept into his voice.

"Are you getting tired, Wally?" Cassiopeia had never heard him talk so much.

"No, no, Cassie. They was a ring Eileen usta have. I kept it after she died, cuz it reminded me of her, and I wanted you to have it, but sis looked all over an can't find it nowheres. If she does though, she's gonna send it on to you. It's that purple stone, you remember?"

Cassiopeia shook her head yes. "I got in big trouble once for wearing it without permission."

"Cassie, did she ever tell you 'bout your daddy?"

Cassiopeia was not prepared for this. Her heart nearly stopped. "You knew about him?"

"Well, what there is to know. Eileen only told me this story once. We was fishin' for cat in the channel. We was visitin' her people down South when you was in Chevyville not long after we was married. I caught me a big old carp 'bout two foot long an give it to this nigra boy. He was tickled pink to get it . . . that thing give me a good ole fight too. Nothin' bitin' after that a tall. Eileen got herself all wired up on black coffee and watchin' that big old moon bobbin' in the channel."

The nurse came in then and took Wally's pulse, blood pressure, and wrote on a clipboard, asking if he needed anything. "Naw, I got everything in the whole world right here . . ." Wally's nod included Cassiopeia. She smiled. "Anyways, she got to talkin'. . . told me how she'd met your father at a carnival in Chicago. Juanita was there with her fella. This guy, Carl Lane, really fell for Eileen, begged her to marry him after just a few dates. He was being shipped overseas in a week. But Eileen was not so sure about it, kept saying no, no. She thought they didn't know each other well enough. But he wouldn't give it up, and two days before he was to leave, the four of them went out on the town, ate at this Chinese restaurant. He'd stuck this ring in a fortune cookie ahead of time, and when Eileen opened hers, well, like she said, she put the ring on and they all went looking for a justice of the peace . . ."

Wally stopped and reached for a glass of water on the bed stand. Cassiopeia could hardly breathe. "Was it the amethyst ring?"

"The purple one. Yep, that's the one. So he ships out, and they write letters, and Eileen gets to feeling all worried and scared. About a month later, he writes and says he's being transported in two weeks, but he can't say where, so she'll just have to wait after that to hear from him. Eileen is feeling now that it's a big mistake, and she tells Juanita that she's going to get the marriage annulled. Juanita begged her not to, but Eileen, well, you know how stubborn she could be . . . she goes down and starts the annullment, and writes him a Dear John letter and sends it off. Course she didn't expect to hear back for awhile, and when she does, it's a letter from the U.S. Government. And now she doesn't know if he got her letter or not. Not long after that, she finds out about you, and like she says to me when she told me the story, 'I'm married, annulled, widowed, and pregnant all in a couple a months time.' After that, she

just flipped out sorta. Wanted to go down and well . . ."
Wally paused. "Stop the pregnancy. She didn't want to
raise a fatherless child . . ."

Cassiopeia didn't move or speak. "She was all
confused like and . . . and . . . rattled."

Cassiopeia detected that these were Wally's
words, not Eileen's. "Did she tell you *all this?*"

"You're pretty smart, Cassie. No, she stopped at
the pregnancy. Juanita told me the other part. It was
Juanita talked her into not doin' nothing rash. And
Juanita too, who told me how that letter ate away at
Eileen's heart for years, her not knowing and all . . .
though Eileen would never say so." Cassiopeia opened
her mouth and found that she couldn't speak at all. Her
face was wet and getting wetter. "Look, Cassie, maybe I
shouldn't have told you all this. Eileen never said not to
but bein' she never told you herself, I held back all this
time . . ."

Cassiopeia found her voice. "No." She paused.
"No, no, no. I can never thank you enough for telling
me. Wally, I needed to know all this. You're a good man
Wally . . . I wish I could have . . ."

Wally interrupted. "I wish I could have . . ." They
both stopped. Cassiopeia put her head on Wally's hos-
pital-gowned chest and sobbed like a little girl.

On the bus on the way home, Cassiopeia stared
unseeing at the chain of fast food and quick stop
stores. She knew now the Eileen that Wally spoke of
was his, not hers. But hers was not real either. The
mother she had carried with her all these years was
one she made up to fit what she knew, but she had
never known it all. "And I still don't," she thought, "and

there's a part I'll never know."

She thought of Wally and of how she thought she'd known him too. The father she had pushed away had given her back her own father — and more. She saw in the window glass the reflection of her own face flashing across the disappearing streets, so enigmatic, so transitory

Chapter 19
•
Chevyville, Illinois

"Is that it?" Hope asked Juanita of every plane that appeared above them until Juanita explained that Cassiopeia's plane would be coming in late at night. But she had given Hope permission to stay up late, if she could do it.

"I can. I can," Hope said, hopping up and down.

They were at the Chevyville cemetery, Juanita with an armful of jonquils. The newer section of the cemetery had carefully clipped lawns and polished granite headstones. It was clean, orderly, and well-kept, just like the suburbs, and far from the truth of the lives sunk beneath it all. Hope and Juanita were in the older section, not nearly so tidy. In fact, some of the stones crumbled, and here and there a few had split in half and tumbled to the ground. But the graves were more interesting here, scalloped stones carved with baby lambs, brooding angels, or a hand with the index finger pointing up through stone flecked with mica like sprinkles of distant stars.

Juanita searched up and down the uneven rows, climbing carefully over the untended ground, looking for a name, it seemed. But when Hope asked who it was that she was looking for, she wouldn't answer. Juanita began to sing, under her breath. "You are my sunshine, my only sunshine. You make me happy, when skies are gray. You'll never know dear, how much I love you. Please don't take my sunshine away."

Hope sat down finally on a grassy hump and watched. Juanita seemed to be circling around Hope's circumference point. A sleepy, honey-colored haze drifted over the graves. The wind whined through the huge, umbrella boughs of ancient sycamores. Hope rolled three purie marbles together in her palm. She'd found them in an old dish at the back of the pantry. Now, they gave off a scraping music as they scumbled together, sunlight bouncing every which way. When she looked up from the puries, Juanita was kneeling, the jonquils sprayed out at the bottom of a small, rectangular stone.

Hope left her perch and wove her way through the grassy mounds to stand beside Juanita, waiting to be noticed. Although she couldn't read, Hope recognized all the letters on the stone and called them out aloud: J-O-H-N-M-A-L-I-C-K. She waited for Juanita to read the name to her or to praise her letters, but Juanita was far from earthly praise and speech and remained silent for a long time. Hope was not the sort of child to persist too long, and she sank to her knees beside Juanita, who had begun to sing again: "You are my sunshine, my only sunshine . . ."

Suddenly a big smile burst across her face as she turned to Hope. "Want to find some of your relatives, Hope?"

Hope was so pleased that she forgot about the mystery grave. She shook her head yes, then followed Juanita, who moved with ease up and around the hill. After a brief search, she stopped at a grave. "Can you read those letters, Hope?"

Hope read: "H-O-M-E-R-I-SAA-C-D-A-V-I-S."

"That's your great grandfather. He died long ago, when your mama's mama was little. Eileen hardly knew him. Course you don't remember your grandma Eileen either, because she died before you were born."

Hope was staring at the mound covered with a silky nap of grass. "Is he really under there?" she asked.

"Oh yes." Juanita started to laugh, then stopped herself, realizing Hope didn't understand what she was saying, had almost no concept of what death meant. "But you understand that he's dead, Hope?"

"Uh huh," said Hope softly, because she knew that adults dropped their voices or whispered when death was mentioned. Her only connection was the time when Cassiopeia had taken her to the zoo with the little girl in the apartment next door to them and Hope had found a dead squirrel on the path to the monkeys' cages. Her sandaled, bare toe had bumped against the quiet bag of fur. Marsella, who was older, let out a shriek and wouldn't stop crying until Cassiopeia promised a hot dog and ice cream. Hope felt both superior to Marsella and peculiarly left out and tried in vain to squeeze out any of her own tears. She whimpered a few times and joined Marsella, hiding her face in Cassiopeia's skirts, but snuck long, fascinated looks.

I saw a squirrel," she said now. "It was real dead. The zoo man came and took it away in a newspaper."

Hope was quiet for several minutes. Then, "Are all the animals under there too, with the people?"

"Uhmm . . . well, yes, they are honey. There's a whole 'nother world down there. No one knows what it's really like."

Hope looked puzzled. "Do they have food? Are they always asleep?"

"No, Hope. They're not asleep, they're dead. It's different, and the world of the dead is different from ours, but we don't know exactly how. And it's hard to imagine, because there's nothing like it we know."

They were both quiet then, Hope thinking of an upside down world where she could walk on the sky, then of the new shoes she'd worn on the plane when she'd come here. Juanita was thinking of Lily. Juanita was not afraid of death. She had met its unblinking stare and stared right back, but this was something else. It was worse than death. As if reading her mind, Hope looked up at her and said, "Is Lily dead, Juanita?"

"No, honey. Well not exactly."

"Can you be sort of dead?"

"Well, she's just not alive like you and I, but she's not dead yet. She's in a dream world, halfway to heaven, I think . . ."

"Is she going to die still?"

"Yes, she probably will."

Hope twisted her hair into a tiny knot. "Maybe she's just resting."

"You know what I think Hope? I think that's quite possible. She's just resting awhile before she moves on. She just couldn't go straight out. I don't know why. I just don't know . . . But everyone who dies leaves us a message you know . . ."

"What was hers?" Hope's eyes grew huge.

"I only have part of it honey, the part she wrote down. She believes she can start over. That's her hope. Maybe she's resting now for a long journey . . . and my job is to find out the rest of the message . . ."

The doctors were feeding Lily intravenously, but she was breathing on her own, and they said there was nothing they could do. Juanita had never felt more powerless in her life. She had found herself unable even to grieve. How could she grieve when Lily was not dead? Most of the doctors were reluctant to discuss Lily's case and gave only the vaguest, most noncommittal replies to any questions. But one, Dr. Ambrose, a huge, bald man who appeared brusque on the surface, had taken her aside and said, "I honestly wish I could tell you more, but in these coma cases, there's just no way to know." He waited then, for Juanita to speak.

"Well, what should I do?"

"I suggest you allow yourself to begin to grieve, and then just go on. Visit this room as if it were her grave, because chances are you won't see her really alive again. I'm telling you this because I'm betting that you are the one who will hold vigil with her."

And he was right. One of the children came, the oldest girl, but Juanita never saw her. She flew in one day and out the next. The youngest boy was in a drug rehab hospital in Arizona, and the middle boy was in the army overseas. And Lester had come with the daughter once but had been rehospitalized after he had started talking of joining Lily, which Juanita didn't believe for a minute. Juanita came every day, sometimes only for a few minutes.

One day, she sat and read aloud from *Alice Through the Looking Glass*, a book that Lily had always loved. When the orderly came in she felt somewhat self-conscious, but he smiled at her knowingly and said, "That's a wonderful idea. Sometimes the sound of a familiar voice helps . . ."

"Yes," Juanita said, "it might help. But don't worry, I have no expectations."

Juanita looked down at Hope now, and thought how she had wanted to try and help Hope understand what was going on and instead Hope had helped her.

The gravestone shadows were beginning to stretch out into oblong blocks that rippled down the hill. The trees were thickening with darker patches, the light melting into buttery yellow pools that fell and slipped away. Juanita stood up, her legs stiff and aching, and took Hope's hand. "There's nothing more we can do here," she said. "Let's leave the dead to their own sorrows. You saw the graves of your ancestors today, Hope. That's very important." In the space of three bird calls, she continued, "Did you know I'm part Indian, Hope?"

Hope shook her head no.

"Uh huh. Iroquois. My people believe that we can't know ourselves until we know our ancestors."

Hope asked quickly then, "Does my mama know them, too."

"Well, not really, I don't think so. But we'll fix that."

They made their way slowly down the sprawling hill, Hope on her own imaginary, upside-down path.

Chapter 20
•
32,000 feet above
the North American continent

Cassiopeia sat looking out the muted, double windows to where the silver wing arched sunlight. She looked around her at the other passengers settling into the cheerful, deodorized seats. The woman one seat over from her was a beauty shop blonde in a white sailor dress with navy purse and pumps. Her stockinged legs gleamed iridescent. Cassiopeia imagined her heels clicking over a polished foyer, speckless gloves blowing kisses to her *House Beautiful* husband and portrait-perfect children just before she slipped smoothly into the cab at the curb. She would have her taxes done in January, her snapshots all dated and captioned in photo albums: "Christian missing his front teeth" or "Cynthia's recital." Or maybe she was nothing like that once you scratched the surface.

Watching the platinum lady adjust her face in her compact and snap it shut, Cassiopeia remembered Eileen's white linen traveling suit with navy piping, the red, sling-back pumps laid out on the bed. Eileen, happy, circled in a golden nimbus of light, the bathroom mirror foamy with steam. She wiped the mirror with her palm so she could trace her bow-shaped pout with cherry red lipstick, blot it on a tissue, and draw a thick brown crescent over each eye. Then came the close up adjustments, leaning into the glass: teeth checked for specks of food, rouge feathered out, a ritual of facial contortions. She would sing then, *Sunny Side of the Street*, or *Frankie and Johnnie*, the bathroom air thick with steam and layers of dusting powder.

Eileen sat on the pearlized commode seat unrolling nylon stockings up to her thighs. She pointed her toes and fastened garters into the dark band at the top. In her stockinged feet, seams were straightened, the toes aligned, ending in two dark peaks. Cassiopeia followed her every gesture, every posture, as if Eileen were a priestess performing a secret ceremony, which in a way, she was.

They were taking the train from Chicago to Memphis and the almost religious preparations had gone on now for weeks: a new plaid dress with ruffled bib, lace cuffed anklets and patent leather shoes with buttons for Cassiopeia. They would buy their meals on the train, and Cassiopeia slipped the silver coin with the angel's outspread wings in and out of her patent leather pocketbook. Of the train ride, Cassiopeia remembered very little: smoke curling up from Eileen's enameled nails when they sat in the smoking car, falling asleep in the train's hypnotic clack and sway. She remembered waking once to a window of stars that slid away and back into themselves. In a flurry of hugging and smeared lipstick, Vangie and Grady met them at the station.

Cassiopeia remembered being puzzled by Vangie and Eileen's tears. Grady smelled of tobacco and Wild Turkey, yawned a lot, and said he'd been up all night with a sick hound pup. Vangie mimed the word "bitch" behind his back, raised the beams of her arched brows and sucked in her cheeks. Eileen was full of questions about this one and that one in the family, and she and Vangie filled the car ride home with their talk. Cassiopeia drooped against the scratchy arm rest. Vangie had pinched and called her cutie at first, but gradually she was ignored in favor of the essence of family gossip.

The night was huge with crickets and mown hay smells as they headed out of the city and followed the moon. As they pulled into the gravel driveway, the roosters crowed up the day and light poured over the horizon's ledge. That was their first trip of any distance, and now Cassiopeia struggled to remember details but it was all somewhat mushy: a chicken slicing her forefinger open when she reached for its freckled eggs, a stream of relatives that circulated through the humid drawl of days clinking tall glasses of iced tea laced with sugar against false teeth, Vangie posing for pictures on a sawhorse with a cowgirl hat and drawn six-shooters.

Or maybe it was only the photos Cassiopeia remembered. She had confused memory and snapshots before. She thought of them as fragments of time, moments trapped in silver, captured later in an album to be studied and filed in the same undusted corner of the mind with memories. And when she looked at the pictures later, the smell of red mud, chicken dung, and fried bacon mornings filled her again. She remembered the row of plum preserves on Vangie's sill, where the summer was sealed tight and waiting to be released the way a pungent smell sets loose a surge of memories. Somewhere in a box, stored at Juanita's were the old snapshots. She would try to find them.

How quickly the past becomes the future, she thought, which then becomes the past even as we think it. Perhaps memories were not meant to be any more real than any other myths.

The stewardesses were snapping shut overhead compartments, breezing busily up and down the aisles tucking in the passengers. Jet engines shuddered, the no smoking bell repeated its pleasant ding. Cassiopeia's stomach lurched as if the bottom dropped out. A swarm of details surged through the terminals of her brain as if released by this sudden velocity. Over it all, loomed the magical, most unbelievable fact that she would soon be with Hope. She wondered why it had taken this long.

"I guess I had to stop fighting so hard," she told Juanita on the phone. "Once I sat still for awhile and looked at the pieces, the picture began to fall into place. Anyway, I want to start over somehow. It's like connecting the dots. It was there all along, but I had to go from this point to that to create the picture."

"I don't know what you're talking about exactly," said Juanita, "but I got plenty of room for you both till you get your life back on course." Then she stopped talking, and Cassiopeia could hear only the crackle and buzz of distance.

"Are you still there, Juanita?"

"Did you say start over?"

"Well, yea, I did . . . why?"

"Well, that's just uncanny. . . . anyway, I'll tell you when you get here. We got a lot to talk about."

Cassiopeia spent the four days after her visit to Wally making arrangements to leave. First she'd gone into the Satellite and resigned. It had not been easy telling Marie, but she had been happy to hear her plans and had attached two twenty dollar bills to her check and a note saying, "Buy some shoes to wear on your trip. And throw those silver killer heels in the trash."

It had not been easy either, to say goodbye to Zona. Cassiopeia had driven out to the hospital and found Zona in a stormy cloud of pain, a cast up to her knee. She'd fractured her ankle playing volleyball and was giving everybody hell. Gail was in Europe "with her latest gigolo," according to Zona. That explained why Cassiopeia had not been able to reach her and had to leave the house key with Marie, who promised to go by several times a week, feed the cat, and keep the place up.

"I'm still checkin' outa this sadistic hotel," Zona said. "You just watch me." But Cassiopeia had a feeling it would be a while yet. Before she left, Cassiopeia promised to bring Hope back for a visit. "Look, Cassie, if you can't afford it, don't go playing proud. Gail can pay your way. One less diamond nose stud for her gigolo. And I just gotta see that little shortcake. I sure miss her."

When Cassiopeia jingled her keys to leave, Zona became uncommonly quiet and looked almost frightened. Cassiopeia said nothing and waited. Finally Zona said, "Cassie, I have a huge favor to ask of you."

"Sure, just name it." Zona seemed surprised.

"Could I be honorary godmother to Hope? I mean, there's no law says she can't have two godmothers is there?"

"If there is, we are gonna be the first to break it." In her last piece of business, Cassiopeia called a lawyer, who said she could take care of the divorce even with Cassiopeia out of the state. Cassiopeia called to tell Ned, wondering after she'd hung up if maybe she'd been calling to say goodbye. Ned's answering machine had come on with a few guitar licks, a neighing horse, and Ned's drowsy voice telling the caller to leave a message and he'd write it on the wall. At the last minute, Cassiopeia had left Juanita's number for Ned to reach her.

"Maybe they need a librarian in Chevyville," Cassiopeia thought, smiling to herself, tilting back in the seat, her eyelids closing against the swirl of clouds that tumbled by like schools of puffy fish. They were now "cruising at 32,000 feet," the captain reported. She looked down between the clouds to a warm, green patchwork quilt spread snugly over the stretched out farmlands. Too heavy now to lift, her eyelids closed while the plane rocked like a basket and the warmth of the sun swept through windows and closed over her like a soft woolen coverlet.

This moment was a Möbius strip twirling in the wind, a carnival ride back and forth between the past and future. She stepped on and off, passed through a body of water, or the body passed over her, she couldn't be sure, lapping and lulling her in a muffled song. Now under the crescent moon, rocking. The cradle turned. Now she curled inside, watching the sky dip and curve away. Now there was a dark moon that floated with her, tugged and brought her back. Now it pulsed up to the top of the sky. She laughed. A little dog followed her through sun and shade. Someone else's pet. Now it nipped at her heels when she began to climb the rungs of a ladder propped against the rain.

Cassiopeia opened her eyes. Slivers of rain were striking the oval windows. Thunder rumbled as if it were directly under the plane. She heard a crack and then saw a splintering flash and the window lit up. The pilot announced they were directly over Kansas, and not to be alarmed. They were well above the lightning and thunderstorms now criss-crossing the midwest. Cassiopeia's leg had fallen asleep and tingled disturbingly. In bare feet, she padded down the aisle to the rear of the plane to where a bigger window opened to another fiery fork of lightning below. She watched it skitter across the black abyss of the continent. She nearly stopped breathing, more fascinated than afraid. In jagged tongues, the lightning licked from one state to the next.

Cassiopeia felt privileged and minute at the same time, like a speck of dust, caught in the pupil of God's eye. A child, probably about Hope's age, was sobbing near the front of the plane in regular, measured wails that the mother tried to shush and soothe away. In a few hours she would be with Hope, would begin to begin again.

She laughed to herself, thinking of the fortune teller's assistant's orders to "assume her true identity."

"Maybe I should take a new name," she thought.

"Quinlan is Ned's name, and Lane is the name I grew up using, but it belonged to a man I'd never known, buried somewhere far across the sea." Maybe she would use Davis, Eileen's maiden name. Cassiopeia and Hope Davis. It didn't sound bad. It was a small thing, this business of a name, but Eileen had spent her life searching for hers.

A new thought crept in, something she had just figured out, something Eileen had never known.

"She could have been enough. If only she had known it. She didn't need to give me a father. And I can be enough. I just have to create myself, the way I used to know how to do when I was that princess cowgirl, when imagining and becoming blended together."

Cassiopeia Davis. Just words. And like the word *tree*, they stood for a particular piece of matter, an arrangement of molecules and the spaces between so the name signified the freckled flesh, the history of dominant and recessive traits, the DNA strand of the particlar bough and branch and twig on a particular spot of the family tree.

Another golden whip of lightning interrupted her thoughts, struck downward illuminating a toy mountain range. Back in her seat, the after-image trembled behind her closed eyelids like a negative, a semblance of the thing itself but really a stimulated spot in the brain, mere reminder of something bigger. The silver dot in the sky that was their plane appeared to the observer below to hang in shimmering limbo, while, in fact, it continued on its charted course, blasting at breathtaking speeds into the violent eye of the storm that was the future.